ELSIE'S
NEW RELATIONS

The Original

ELSIE DINSMORE

COLLECTION

Elsie Dinsmore

Elsie's Holidays at Roselands

Elsie's Girlhood

Elsie's Womanhood

Elsie's Motherhood

Elsie's Children

Elsie's Widowhood

Grandmother Elsie

Elsie's New Relations

Elsie at Nantucket

The Two Elsies

Elsie's Kith and Kin

Elsie's Friends at Woodburn

Christmas with Grandma Elsie

Elsie and the Raymonds

Elsie Yachting with the Raymonds

Elsie's Vacation

Elsie at Viamede

Elsie at Ion

Elsie at the World's Fair

Elsie's Journey on Inland Waters

Elsie at Home

Elsie on the Hudson

Elsie in the South

Elsie's Young Folks

Elsie's Winter Trip

Elsie and Her Loved Ones

Elsie and Her Namesakes

ELSIE'S
NEW RELATIONS

Book Nine

Martha Finley

HENDRICKSON
PUBLISHERS

Elsie's New Relations

Hendrickson Publishers Marketing, LLC
P. O. Box 3473
Peabody, Massachusetts 01961-3473

ISBN 978-1-59856-408-2

Printed in the United States of America, by Versa Press, East Peoria, Illinois

Original publication date—1877

First Hendrickson Edition Printing—February 2010

Chapter First

For wild, or calm, or far or near,
I love thee still, thou glorious sea.

— Mrs. Hemans

I bless thee for kind looks and words
Shower'd on my path like dew,
For all the love in those deep eyes,
A gladness ever new.

— Mrs. Hemans

*I*t was late in the afternoon of a delicious October day. The woods to the back of the two cottages where the Dinsmores, Travillas, and Raymonds had spent the last three or four months were clothed with scarlet, crimson, and gold. The air from the sea was more delightful than ever, but the summer visitors to the neighboring cottages and hotels had fled, and the beach was almost deserted as Edward and his wife wandered slowly along it, hand in hand. Their attention was divided between the splendors of a magnificent sunset and the changing beauty of the sea. Yonder away in the distance it was a pale grey, near at hand a delicate green slowly changing to pink, each wave crested with snowy foam, and anon they all turned to a brilliant, burnished gold.

"Oh, how very beautiful!" cried Zoe, in an ecstasy of delight. "Edward, have you ever seen anything finer in all your life?"

"Never! Let us go down this flight of steps and seat ourselves on the next to the lowest. We will then be quite near the waves and yet out of danger of being wet by them."

He led her down as he spoke, seating his wife comfortably and himself by her side with his arm lightly around her.

"I've grown very fond of the sea," she remarked. "I shall be very sorry to leave it. Will you not be sorry to leave it?"

"Yes and no," he answered, doubtfully. "I, too, am fond of the ocean, but I am also eager to get to Ion and begin life in earnest. Isn't it time, seeing I have been a married man for nearly five months? Ah, but why that sigh, love?"

"Oh, Edward, are you not sorry you are married? Are you not sometimes very much ashamed of me?" she asked, her cheeks burning hotly and the downcast eyes filling with tears.

"Ashamed of you, Zoe? Why, darling, you are my heart's best treasure," he said, drawing her closer to his side and touching his lips to her forehead. "What has put so absurd an idea into your head?"

"I know so little, so very little compared to your mother and sisters," she sighed. "I'm finding it out more and more every day, as I hear them talk among themselves and to other people."

"But you are younger than any of them, a very great deal younger than mamma, and you will have plenty of time to catch up to them."

"But I'm a married woman and can't go to school any more. Ah," with another and very heavy sigh, "I wish papa hadn't been quite so indulgent, or that I'd had sense enough not to take advantage of it to the neglect of my studies!"

"No, I suppose it would hardly do to send you to school, even if I could spare you—which I can't," he returned laughingly, "but there is a possibility of studying at home, under a governess or tutor. What do you say to offering yourself as a pupil to grandpa?"

"Oh, no, no! I'm sure he can be very stern upon occasion. I've seen it in his eyes when I've made a foolish remark that he didn't approve, and I should be too frightened to learn if he were my teacher."

"Then someone else must be thought of," Edward said with a look of amusement. "How would I do?"

"You? Oh, splendidly!"

"You are not afraid of me?"

"No, indeed!" she cried with a merry laugh and a saucy look up into his face.

"And yet, I'm the only person who has authority over you."

"Authority, indeed!" she said with quite a little contemptuous sniff.

"You promised to obey, you know."

"Did I? Well, maybe so, but that's just a form that doesn't really mean anything. Most any married woman will tell you that."

"Do you consider the whole of your marriage vow an unmeaning form, Zoe?" he asked with sudden gravity and a look of doubt and pain in his eyes that she could not bear to see.

"No! I was only in jest," she said dropping her eyes and blushing. "But really, Edward, you don't think, do you, that wives are to obey like children?"

"No, love, I don't. I think in a true marriage the two are so entirely one—so unselfishly desirous each to please the other—that there is little or no clashing of wills. Thus far, ours has seemed such to me. How is it, do you think, little wife?"

"I hope so, Edward," she said, laying her head on his shoulder. "I know one thing—that there is nothing in this world I care so much for as to please you and be all and everything to you."

"And I can echo your words from my very heart, dearest," he said, caressing her. "I hope you are at home and happy among your new relatives."

"Yes, indeed, Edward, especially with mamma. She is the dearest, kindest mother in the world—to me as much as to her own children—and oh, so wise and good!"

"You are not sorry now that you and I are not to live alone?" he queried, with a pleased smile.

"No, oh, no! I'm ever so glad that she is to keep house at Ion and all of us to live together as one big family."

"Except Lester and Elsie," he corrected. "They will be with us for a short time, then go to Fairview for the winter. And it will probably become their home after that, for mamma will buy it, if Mr. Leland—Lester's uncle, who owns the place—carries out his intention of moving to California. His children have settled there, and, of course, the father and mother want to be near them."

The sun had set, and all the bright hues had faded from the sea, leaving it a dull grey.

"What a deserted spot this seems!" remarked Zoe, "and only the other day it was happy with crowds of people. Nobody to be seen now but ourselves," glancing up and down the coast as she spoke. "Ah, yes! Yonder is someone sitting on that piece of wreck."

"Why, it is Lulu," Edward said, following the direction of her glance. "It is late for the child to be out so far from home—a full mile I should say. I'll go and invite her to walk back with us."

"No, you needn't," said Zoe, "for see, there is her father going to her. But let us go home, for I must change my dress before tea."

"And I want to walk leisurely along," returned Edward rising and giving her his hand to help her up the steps.

Lulu was reading, so absorbed in the story that she did not perceive her father's approach. As he accosted her with, "It is late for you to be here alone, my child; you should have come in an hour ago," she gave a great start, and involuntarily tried to hide her book.

"What have you there? Evidently something you do not wish your father to see," he said, bending down and taking it from her unwilling hand.

"Ah, I don't wonder!" he said as he hurriedly turned over a few pages. "A dime novel! Where did you get this, Lulu Raymond?"

"It's Max's, papa; he lent it to me. Oh, papa, what made you do that?" she cried, as with an great fling, the captain suddenly sent it far out into sea. "Max made me promise to take care of it and give it back to him, and besides, I wanted to finish the story."

"Neither you nor Max shall ever again read such poisonous stuff as that with my knowledge and consent," replied the captain in stern accents.

"Papa, I didn't think you could be so unkind," grumbled Lulu, her face expressing extreme vexation and disappointment. "Or that you would throw away other people's things."

"Unkind, my child?" he said, sitting down beside her and taking her hand in his. "Suppose you had gathered a quantity of beautiful, sweet-tasting berries that I knew to be poisonous, and you were about to eat them. Would it be unkind of me to snatch them out of your hand and throw them into the sea?"

"No, sir, because it would kill me to eat them; but that book couldn't kill me, or even make me sick."

"No, not your body, but it would injure your soul, which is worth far more. I'm afraid I have been too negligent in regard to the mental food of my children," he went on after a slight pause, rather as if thinking aloud than talking to Lulu. "And unfortunately I cannot take the oversight of it constantly in the future. But, remember, Lulu," he added firmly, "I wholly forbid dime novels, and you are not to read anything without first obtaining the approval of your father or one of those under whose authority he has placed you."

Lulu's face was full of sullen discontent and anger. "Papa," she said, "I don't like to obey those people instead of you."

"If you are wise, you will try to like what has to be," he said.

"It wouldn't have to be if you would only say I needn't, papa."

"I shall not say that, Lucilla," he answered with grave displeasure. "You need guidance and control even more than most children of your age, and I should not be doing my duty as your father if I left you without them."

"I don't like to obey people that are no relation to me!" she cried, viciously kicking away a little heap of sand.

"No, you don't even like to obey your father," he said with a sigh. "Max and Gracie together do not give me half the anxiety that you do by your willful temper, Lulu."

"Why can't I do as I please like grown people?" she asked in a more subdued tone.

"Even grown people have to obey," said her father. "I am now expecting orders from the government, and I must obey them when they come. I must obey my superior officers, and the officers and men under me must obey me. So must my children. God gave you to me and requires me to train you up in His fear and service to the best of my ability. I should not be doing that if I allowed you to read such hurtful trash as that I just took from you."

"It was Max's, papa, and I promised to give it back. What shall I say when he asks me for it?"

"Tell him to come to me about it."

"Papa—"

"Well, what is it, my little Lu?" he asked, as she paused and hesitated.

"Please, papa, don't punish him. You never told him not to buy or read such things, did you?"

"No, and I think he would not have done so in defiance of a prohibition from me. So I shall not punish him. But I am pleased that you should plead for him. I am very glad that my children all love and care for one another."

"Yes, indeed we do, papa!" she said. "And we all love you, and you love Max and Gracie very much, and you—"

"And Lulu also," he said putting his arm about her and drawing her closer to his side, as she paused with quivering lip and downcast eyes.

"As much as you do Max and Gracie?" she asked brokenly, hiding her face on his shoulder. "You said just now I was naughtier than both of them."

"Yet, you are my own dear child, and it is because I love you so dearly that I am so distressed over your quick temper and willfulness. I fear that if not conquered they will cause great unhappiness to yourself as well as to your friends. I want you to promise me, daughter, that you will try to conquer them, asking God to help you."

"I will, papa," she said with unwonted humility, "but, oh, I wish you were going to stay with us! It's easier to be good with you than with anybody else."

"I am sorry, indeed, that I cannot," he said, rising and taking her hand. "Come, we must go back to the house now."

They moved along in silence for a little, then Lulu said with an affectionate look up into her father's face, "Papa, I do so like to walk this way!"

"How do you mean?" he asked, smiling kindly down upon her.

"With my hand in yours, papa. You know I haven't often had this chance."

"No, my poor child," he sighed, "that is one of the deprivations to which a seaman and his family have to submit."

"Well," she said, lifting his hand to her lips, "I'd rather have you for my father than anybody else."

At that, with a smile full of pleasure and fatherly affection, he bent down and kissed his daughter.

Chapter Second

By thy words thou shalt be justified,
and by thy words thou shalt be condemned.

— MATTHEW 12:37

As they drew near the house Max hurried out to meet them.

"I've been to the post office since the mail came in, papa," he said, "and there is no government letter for you, yet. I'm so glad!! I hope they're going to let us keep you a good deal longer."

"I'm not sorry to prolong my stay with my wife and children," the captain responded, "but cannot hope to be permitted to do so very much longer."

"Grandpa Dinsmore has come back from taking Harold and Herbert to college," pursued Max, "and we're all to take tea there, Mamma Vi says—because grandpa wants us all about him this first evening."

"That is kind," said the captain, opening the gate and looking smilingly at Violet, who, with little Gracie, was waiting for him on the veranda. He stopped there to speak with them, while Lulu hurried on into the house and up to her own room, Max following.

"Where's my book, Lu?" he asked.

"Oh, Max, I'm sorry, but I couldn't help it—papa caught me reading it and took it away from me. And he told me when you asked me for it I should send you to him."

Max's face expressed both vexation and alarm. "I sha'n't do that," he said, "if I never get it. But was he very angry, Lu?"

"No, and you needn't be afraid to go to him, for he won't punish you. I asked him not to, and he said he wouldn't. But he threw the book into the sea, and said neither you nor I should ever read such poisonous stuff with his knowledge or consent."

"Then, where would be the use of my going to him for it? I'll not say a word about it."

He went out, closed the door behind him, and stood irresolutely in the hall, debating with himself whether to go upstairs or down. Upstairs in his room was another dime novel that he had been reading that afternoon. He had not quite finished it and was eager to do so. He wanted very much to know how the story ended, and had meant to read the few remaining pages now before the call to tea. But his father's words, reported to him by Lulu, made it disobedience.

It's a very little sin, whispered the tempter. *Having read so much of the story, you may as well read the rest.*

But it will be disobeying willfully the kind father who forgave a heedless act of disobedience not very long ago, said conscience, *the dear father who must soon leave you to be gone no one knows how long, perhaps never to come back.*

Just then the captain came quickly up the stairs. "Ah, Max, there you are," he said in a cheery tone, then laid his hand affectionately on the boy's shoulder. "Come in here with me, my son; I want to have a little talk with you while I get ready for tea."

"Yes, sir," said Max immediately following him into the dressing room.

"What have you been reading today?" asked the captain, throwing off his coat, pouring water into the basin from the pitcher, and beginning to wash.

Max hung his head in silence until the question was repeated, then stammered out the title of the book—the one he was so desirous to finish.

"Where did you get it?" asked the father.

"I bought it at a newsstand, papa."

"You must not buy anything more of that kind, Max. You must not read any such trash."

"I will not again, papa. I should not this time if you had ever forbidden me before."

"No, I don't believe you would be guilty of willful disobedience to any positive command of your father," the captain said in a grave but kindly tone. "And, yet, I think you suspected I would not approve. Why else would you be so unwilling to tell me what you had been reading just now?"

He was standing before the bureau now, hairbrush in hand, and as he spoke, he paused in his work and gazed searchingly at his son.

Max's face flushed hotly and his eyes drooped for a moment, then looking up into his father's face he said frankly, "Yes, papa, I believe I was afraid you might take the book from me if you saw it. I deserve that you should be angry with me for that and for lending one to Lu."

"I am displeased with you on both accounts," the captain replied, "but I shall overlook it this time, my son, hoping there will be no repetition of either offense. Now go to your room, gather up all the doubtful reading matter you have, and bring it here to me. I shall not go with you but trust your honor to keep nothing back."

"Oh, thank you, papa, for trusting me!" cried Max, his countenance brightening wonderfully, and he hastened away to do his father's bidding.

"Just the dearest, kindest father that ever was!" he said to himself as he bounded up the stairs. "I'll never do anything again to vex him, if I can help it."

He was down again in a moment's time with two dime novels and a story paper of the same stamp.

The captain had finished dressing. Seating himself, he took what Max had brought and glancing hastily over it, "How much of this trash have you read, Max?" he asked.

"The paper and most of one book, papa. I'll not read any more such, since you've forbidden me, but they're very interesting, papa."

"I dare say, to a boy of your age. But you don't think I would deprive you of any innocent pleasure, do you, Max?"

"No, sir, oh, no! But may I know why you won't let me read such stories?"

"Yes, it is because they give false views of life, and thus lead to wrong and foolish actions. Why, Max, some boys have been made burglars and highwaymen by such stories. I want you to be a reader, but of good and wholesome literature—books that will give you useful information and good moral teachings. Above all things, my son, I would have you a student of the Bible, the Holy Scriptures, 'which are able to make you wise unto salvation through faith which is in Jesus Christ.' Do you read it often, Max?"

"Not very, papa. But you know I hear you read it every morning and evening."

"Yes, but I have sometimes been grieved to see that you paid very little attention."

Max colored at that. "Papa, I will try to do better," he said.

"I hope you will," said his father. "You will enjoy the same religious advantages at Ion, and, my boy, try to profit by them, remembering that we shall have to render an account at the last of the use or abuse of all our privileges. I want you to promise me that you will read a few verses of the Bible every day, and commit at least one to memory."

"I will, papa. And what else shall I read? You will let me have some storybooks, won't you?" Max asked entreatingly.

"Yes," said his father, "I have no objection to stories of the right sort. There are some beautiful stories in the Bible; there are entertaining stories in history; and there are fictitious stories that will do you good and not harm. I shall take care in the future that you have plenty of wholesome mental food so that you will have no excuse for craving such stuff as this," he added with a glance of disgust at what he held in his hand. "It may go into the kitchen fire."

"Mrs. Scrimp never burned the least little bit of paper, papa," said Max.

"Indeed! Why not?" asked the father with an amused smile.

"She says it is wicked waste, because it is better than rags for the paper makers."

"Ah! Well, then, we will tear these into bits and let them go to the paper makers."

Max was standing by his father's side. "Papa," he said with a roguish look into his father's face, "don't you think you might enjoy reading them first, yourself?"

The captain laughed. "No, my son," he said. "I have not the slightest inclination to read them. Bring me that waste basket and you may help me tear them up."

They began the work of destruction—Max taking the paper, the captain the book his son had been reading. Presently something in it attracted his attention. He paused and glanced over several pages one after the other, till Max began to think he had become interested in the story. But no—at that instant he turned from it to him and Max was frightened at the sternness of his look.

"My son," he said, "I am astonished and deeply grieved that you could read and enjoy anything like this, for it is full of profanity. Reading or hearing such expressions is very likely to lead to the use of them. Max, do you ever say such words?"

Max trembled and grew red and pale by turns, but did not speak.

"Answer me," was his father's stern command.

"Not often, papa."

The captain barely caught the low-breathed words. "Not often? Sometimes, then?" he groaned, covering his face with his hand.

"Oh, papa, don't be so grieved! I'll never do it again," Max said in a broken voice.

The captain sighed deeply. "Max," he said, "dearly as I love my only son, I would sooner lay him under the sod, knowing that his soul was in heaven, than have him live to be a profane swearer. Bring me that Bible from the table yonder."

The boy obeyed.

"Now, turn to the twenty-fourth chapter of Leviticus and read the sixteenth verse."

Max read in a trembling voice, "'And he that blasphemeth the name of the Lord, he shall surely be put to death, and all the congregation shall certainly stone him; as well the stranger, as he that is born in the land, when he blasphemeth the name of the Lord, shall be put to death.'"

"Now the twenty-third," said his father.

"'And Moses spake to the children of Israel, that they should bring forth him that had cursed out of the camp, and stone him with stones; and the children of Israel did as the Lord commanded Moses.'"

Max had some difficulty in finishing the verse and at the end broke down.

"Papa," he sobbed, "I didn't know that was in the Bible. I never thought about its being so dreadfully wicked to say bad words."

"What do you think a boy deserves who has done it again and again? Say as often as Max Raymond has?" asked his father.

"I suppose to be stoned to death like that man. But nobody is ever put to death for swearing nowadays," the boy said, half inquiringly, not daring to look at his father as he spoke.

"No, Max, fortunately for you and many others. But suppose you were my father and I a boy of your age, and that I had been swearing. What would you think you ought to do about it?"

"Give him a sound flogging," he answered in a low, reluctant tone.

"Well, Max, that is just what I shall have to do, if I ever know you to use a profane word again," said the father in a grave, sad tone. "I should do it now, but for the hope that you are sorry enough for the past to carefully avoid that sin in the future."

"Indeed I will, papa," he said very humbly.

"And, Max," resumed his father, "you are never to make a companion of, or go at all with, anybody who uses such language, and never to read a book or story that has in it anything of the kind. And you are not to say 'by George' or 'by anything.' Our Savior says, 'Let your communication be yea, yea, nay, nay, for whatsoever is more than these cometh of evil.' My son, have you asked God to forgive you for taking His holy name in vain?"

"No, sir."

"Then go at once to your room and do it."

"I did, papa," Max said when he came down again to find his father waiting for him.

"I trust the petition came from your heart, my son," was the grave but kind rejoinder. "I must have a little more talk with you on this subject, but not now, for it is time we followed the others into the next house if we would not keep Grandma Rose's tea waiting."

Chapter Third

A kingdom is a nest of families,
and a family is a small kingdom.

— TUPPER

*I*t was a bright and cheerful scene that greeted the eyes of Captain Raymond and his son as they entered the parlor of the adjacent cottage.

It was strictly a family gathering, yet, the room was quite full. Mr. Dinsmore was there with his wife, his daughter Elsie, Edward and Zoe, Elsie Leland with her husband and babe, Violet Raymond with her husband's two little girls, Lulu and Gracie, and lastly Rosie and Walter.

Everybody had a kindly greeting for the captain, and Violet's bright face grew still brighter as she made room for him on the sofa by her side.

"We were beginning to wonder what was keeping you," she said.

"Yes, I'm afraid I am rather behind time," he returned. "I hope you have not delayed your tea for me, Mrs. Dinsmore."

"No, it is but just ready," she said. "Ah, there's the bell. Please, all of you walk out."

When the meal was over all returned to the parlor, where they all spent the next hour in desultory chat.

Gracie claimed a seat on her father's knee. Lulu took possession of an ottoman and pushed it up as close to his side as she could, then seating herself upon it, leaned up against him.

He smiled and stroked her hair, then glanced about the room in search of Max.

The boy was sitting silently in a corner, but reading an invitation in his father's eyes, he rose and came to his other side.

The ladies were each talking of the clothing and household purchases they wished to make in Boston, New York, or Philadelphia on their homeward route.

"I must get winter hats for Lulu and for Gracie," said Violet.

"I would like a bird on mine, Mamma Vi," said Lulu, "a pretty one with bright feathers."

"Do you know, Lulu, that they skin the poor little birds alive in order to preserve the brilliancy of their plumage?" Violet said with a troubled look. "I will not wear them on that account, and as you are a kind-hearted little girl, I think you will not wish to do so either."

"But I do," persisted Lulu. "Of course, I wouldn't have a bird killed on purpose, but after they are killed I might just as well have one."

"But do you not see," said Grandma Elsie, "that if everyone would refuse to buy them, the cruel business of killing them could soon cease. But it will go on as long as people continue to buy and wear them, Lulu?"

"I don't care. I want one," pouted Lulu. "Papa, can't I have it?"

"No, you cannot," he said with grave displeasure. "I am sorry to see that you can be so heartless. You may have whatever Grandma Elsie and Mamma Vi think best for you, and with that you must be content, young lady."

Lulu was silenced, but for the rest of the evening her face wore an ugly scowl.

"My little girl is growing sleepy," the captain said presently to Gracie. "Papa will carry you home and put you to bed. Lulu, you may come, too."

"I don't want to, papa, I—" she began, but he silenced her with a look.

"Bid good night to our friends and come," he said. "You also, Max."

Max, though surprised by the order, obeyed with cheerful alacrity in strong contrast to Lulu's sullen and reluctant compliance, that said as plainly as words that she would rebel if she dared.

"I don't see why papa makes us come away so soon," she grumbled to her brother in an undertone as they passed from one cottage to the other, their father a little in advance.

"He must have some good reason," said Max. "And I for one am willing enough to obey him, seeing it's such a little thing while I'll have the chance."

They had now reached the veranda of their own little cottage.

"Come in quickly out of this cold wind, my children," their father said. Then, as he closed the outer door after them, he said, "Run into the parlor and get thoroughly warm before going up to your rooms."

He sat down by the stove with Grace on his knee and bade the other two to draw up close to it and him, one on each side. And when they had done so, "My three children," he said in tender tones, glancing from one to another, "no words can tell how much I love you. Will you all think very often of papa and follow him with your prayers when he is far away on the sea?"

"Oh, yes, yes, papa!" they all said with tears in their eyes, while Gracie put her small arms round his neck, Lulu rested her head on his shoulder, and Max took a hand and pressed it in both of his.

"Papa, you will think of us, too?" Max inquired.

"Yes, indeed, my darlings. You will never be long out of my mind, and nothing will make me happier than to hear that you all are well and doing your duty faithfully."

"I shall try very hard, papa," Max said with an affectionate look and tone. "If it is only to please you and make your heart glad."

"Thank you, my son," his father replied, "but I hope a still stronger motive will be that you may please God and honor Him. Never forget, my children, that though your earthly father may be far away and know nothing of your conduct, God's all-seeing eye is ever upon you."

The next half hour passed very quickly and delightfully to the children. At length, upon seeing Gracie's eyelids begin to droop, their father said it was time for him to carry her up to bed.

"Shall we stay here till you come down again, papa?" asked Max.

"No, you and Lulu may go to bed now."

"Then good night, papa."

"No, you need not bid me good night, yet," the captain said. "I shall see you both in your rooms before you are asleep."

"Well, Lu, are you sorry now that papa made you come home so soon?" asked Max as they went upstairs together.

"No, indeed! Haven't we had a nice time, Max? Oh, if only we could keep papa all the time!"

"I wish we could," said Max. "But we won't have so hard a time as we've had for the last two years whenever he was away."

They had reached the door to Lulu's room. "Max," she said turning to him with a sudden thought, "what do you suppose papa is coming to our rooms for?"

"What do you suppose? Have you done anything you ought to be punished for?" asked Max a little mischievously. "I thought you looked cross and rebellious about the hat and about having to come home so soon. I'm very sure, from what I've heard of Grandpa Dinsmore's strictness, that if you were his child you'd get a whipping for it."

Lulu looked frightened. "But, Max, you don't think papa means to punish me for that, do you? He has been so kind and pleasant since then," she said with a slight tremble in her voice.

"I guess you'll find out when he comes," laughed Max. "Good night," he called as he hastened away to his own room.

A guilty conscience made Lulu very uneasy as she hurried through her preparations for bed, and as she heard her father's step approach the door she grew quite frightened.

He came in and closed it after him. Lulu was standing in her night-gown, just ready for bed. He caught up a heavy shawl, wrapped it about her, and seating himself, lifted her to his knee.

"Why, how you are trembling!" he exclaimed. "What is the matter, my little Lulu? Are you cold, my little darling?"

"Oh, papa! Are you—are you going to punish me for being so naughty this evening?" she asked, hanging her head while her cheeks grew red.

"That was not my intention in coming here," he said. "But, Lulu, your willfulness is a cause of great anxiety to me. I hardly know what to do with you. I am very loath to burden our kind friends—Grandpa Dinsmore and Grandma Elsie—with so rebellious and unmanageable a child, for it will be painful to them to be severe with you, and yet, I see that you will compel them to it."

"I won't be punished by anybody but you! Nobody has the right!" burst out Lulu.

"Yes, my child, I have given them the right, and the only way for you to escape punishment is not to deserve it. And if you prove too troublesome for them, you are to be sent to a boarding school, and that, you must understand, involves separation from Max and Gracie, and life among strangers."

"Papa, you wouldn't, you couldn't be so cruel!" she said bursting into tears and hiding her face on his chest.

"I hope you will not be so cruel to yourself as to make it necessary," he said. "I had fondly hoped you were improving, but your conduct tonight shows me that you are still a self-willed and a rebellious child."

"Well, papa, I've wanted a bird on my hat for ever so long, and I believe you would have let me have it, too, if Mamma Vi and Grandma Elsie hadn't said that."

"I shouldn't let you have it, if they were both in favor of it," he said severely.

"Why, papa?"

"Because of the cruelty it would encourage. And now, Lucilla, I want you to reflect how very kind it is in Grandpa Dinsmore and Grandma Elsie to be willing to take my children in and share with them their own delightful home. You have not the slightest claim upon their kindness, and very few people in their case would have made such an offer. I really feel almost ashamed to accept so much without being able to make some return, even if I knew my children would all behave as dutifully and gratefully as possible. And knowing how likely your conduct is to be the exact reverse of that, I can hardly reconcile it to my conscience to let you go with them to Ion. I am afraid I ought to place you in a boarding school at once, before I am ordered away."

"Oh, papa, please don't!" she begged. "I'll try to behave better."

"You must promise more than that," he said. "Promise me that you will yield to the authority of your mamma and her mother and grandfather as if it were mine—obeying their orders and submitting to any punishment they may see fit to inflict, just as if it were my act."

"Papa, have you said they might punish me?" she asked with a look of wounded pride.

"Yes, I have full confidence in their wisdom and kindness. I know they will not abuse the authority, and I have told them they may use any measures with my children that they would with their own in the same circumstances. Will you promise what I require?"

"Papa, it is too hard!"

"The choice is between that and being sent to boarding school."

"Oh, it's so hard!" she sobbed.

"Not hard at all if you choose to be good," her father said. "In that case you will have a delightful life at Ion. Do you make the promise?"

"Yes, sir," she said, as if the words were wrung from her, then hid her face on his chest again and cried bitterly.

"My little daughter, these are tears of pride and stubbornness," sighed her father, passing his hand caressingly over her hair, "and you will never be happy until those evil passions are cast out of your heart. They are foes with which you must fight and conquer by the help of Him who is mighty to save, or they will cost you the loss of your soul. Any sin unrepented of and unforsaken will drag you down to eternal death. The Bible says, 'Without holiness no man shall see the Lord.'"

"Papa," she said, "you are the only person God commands me to obey, and I'm willing to do that."

"No, it seems not, when my command is that you obey someone else. My little girl, you need something that I cannot give you, and that is a change of heart. Go to Jesus for it, daughter. Ask Him to wash away all your sins in His precious blood and to create in you a clean heart and renew a right spirit within you. He is able and willing to do it, for He says, 'Him that cometh unto me I will in no wise cast out.' We will kneel down and ask Him now."

As they finished, Lulu said, "Papa, I do love you so. I love you dearly, and I will try to be a better girl." Lulu clasped her arms tightly about his neck as he laid her in her bed and bent down to softly kiss her good night.

"I hope so, my darling," he said. "Nothing could make me happier than to know you to be a truly good child, trying to live right that you may please the dear Savior who died that you might live."

Max, lying in his bed, was just saying to himself, "I wonder what keeps papa so long," when he heard his step on the stairs.

"Are you awake, Max?" the captain asked, as he opened the door and came in.

"Yes, sir," was the cheerful response. "It's early, as you know, papa, and I'm not at all sleepy."

"That is well, for I want a little talk with you," said his father, sitting down on the side of the bed and taking Max's hand in his.

The talk was on the sin of profanity. Max was told to repeat the third commandment, then his father called his attention to the words, "The Lord will not hold him guiltless that taketh His name in vain."

"It is a dreadful and dangerous sin, my son," he said, "a most foolish sin, too, for there is absolutely nothing to be gained by it. It is the meanest of sins, for what can be meaner than to abuse Him to whom we owe our being and every blessing we enjoy?"

"Yes, papa, and I—I've done it a good many times. Do you think God will ever forgive me?" Max asked in trembling tones.

"'He that covereth his sins shall not prosper; but whoso confesseth and forsaketh them shall have mercy.' 'I, even I, am He that blotteth out thy transgressions, for Mine own sake, and will not remember thy sins,'" quoted the captain.

"Yes, my own little son, if you are truly sorry for the sins committed against God and confess them with the determination to forsake them, asking forgiveness and help to overcome the evil of your own nature, for Jesus' sake, it will be granted unto you. 'The blood of Jesus Christ, His Son, cleanseth us from all sin.'"

Chapter Fourth

No day discolor'd with domestic strife,
No jealousy, but mutual truth believ'd,
Secure repose and kindness undeceiv'd.

—DRYDEN

They were a bright and cheery company in the other house. They had divided into groups. Mrs. Elsie Travilla sat in a low rocking chair between her father and his wife with her little grandson on her lap. She doted on the babe and was often to be seen with him in her arms. She was now calling her father's attention to his beauty, and talking of the time when his mother was an infant, her own precious darling.

On a sofa on the farther side of the room the two sisters, Elsie and Violet, sat side by side cozily chatting of things past and present, while a little removed from them Lester, Edward, and Zoe formed another group.

The two gentlemen were in quite an animated conversation, to which Zoe was a silent and absorbed listener, especially when her husband spoke. She eagerly drank in every word that fell from his lips—her face glowing, her eyes sparkling with proud delight.

"Look at Zoe. Ned certainly has one devoted admirer," remarked Elsie, regarding her young sister-in-law with a pleased and half-amused smile.

"Yes," said Violet, "he is a perfect oracle in her esteem. And I believe everything she does is right in his eyes. Indeed, their mutual devotion is a pretty thing to see. They are scarcely ever apart."

"Don't you consider your husband an oracle?" asked Elsie with a quizzical look.

"So you have found that out already, have you?" laughed Violet. "Yes, I do, but then he is wiser than our Ned, you know. Tell me now, don't you admire him? Don't you think him worthy of all honor?"

"I do, indeed, and am proud to have him for a brother-in-law," Elsie said with earnest sincerity. "But," she added with a smile, "I certainly prefer Lester for a husband."

"Yes, of course, but Levis is the best of husbands—of fathers, too."

"Rather more strict and stern than ours was, is he not, Violet?"

"Yes, but not more so than necessary with a child of Lulu's peculiar disposition."

"Ah, Vi, I pity you for being a stepmother," Elsie said with a compassionate look at her sister.

"You needn't," returned Violet quickly. "Lulu is the only one of the three that gives me any anxiety or trouble, and to be Captain Raymond's wife more than compensates for that."

"I suppose so. And Gracie is a dear little thing."

"Yes, she's a darling. And Max is a noble fellow. I hope he will make just such a man as his father. Don't you think he resembles the captain in looks?"

"Yes, and I notice he is very chivalrous in his manner toward his young stepmother."

"Yes," Violet said with a happy smile, "and more or less to all ladies, especially those of this family. He is like his father in that. Zoe is, I think, a particular favorite with him."

Evidently Zoe had overheard the remark, for she turned in their direction with a bright look and smile. Then, springing up, came quickly toward them. Taking possession of a low chair near at hand she said, "Was it Max you were talking of, Violet? Yes, indeed, I am fond of him. I think he's a splendid boy. But what was wrong with him tonight?"

"Nothing so far as I know," said Violet. "Why do you think there was?"

"Because he was so unusually quiet, and then his father took him away so early. Ah, here comes the captain now," as the door opened and Captain Raymond entered, "so I'll go away and let you have him to yourself."

"You needn't," said Violet, but Zoe was already by Edward's side again. Elsie, too, rose and went to her mother to ask if she were not weary of holding the babe.

Violet looked up anxiously into her husband's face as she made room for him on the sofa by her side. "Is anything wrong with the children, Levis?" she asked in an undertone.

"No, love," he said, "I took them away early that I might have a little serious talk with the older two. You know I shall not long be afforded the opportunity."

"But you look troubled," she said in tender, sympathizing accents. "May I not share your care or sorrow, whatever it is?"

"I would rather share only joys and blessings with you, dearest, and keep the cares and burdens to myself," he answered, smiling lovingly upon her and pressing with affectionate warmth the little hand she had placed in his.

"No, I can't consent to that," she said. "I consider it one of my precious privileges to be allowed to share your burdens and anxieties. Won't you tell me what troubles you?"

"It is nothing new, little wife," he answered cheerfully, "but I am doubting whether I do right to give your mother and grandfather so troublesome a charge as Lulu. She is almost certain to be willful and rebellious occasionally, if not oftener."

Mrs. Travilla had resigned the babe to his mother and was now standing near the sofa where the captain and Violet sat.

"Mamma," said the latter, turning to her, "my husband is making himself absolutely miserable with the fear that Lulu will prove too troublesome to you and grandpa."

"Please, do not, captain," Elsie said brightly, accepting the easy chair he hastened to bring forward for her. "Why should I not have a little trouble as well as other people? Lulu is an attractive child to me, very bright and original, a little headstrong, perhaps, but I shall lay siege to her heart and try to rule her through her affections."

"I think that may be the better plan," he said, the look of care lifting from his brow. "She is a warm-hearted child, and more easily led than driven. But she is sometimes very impertinent, and I would by no means have her indulged in that. I wish you would promise me never to let it pass without punishment. She must be taught respect for authority and for her superiors."

Elsie's face had grown very grave while he was speaking. "What punishment do you prescribe?" she asked. "The child is yours."

"That should depend upon the heinousness of the offense," he replied. "I can only say, please treat her exactly as if she were your own."

Mr. and Mrs. Dinsmore now joined them and the question of what studies the children should pursue during the coming winter was discussed and settled. Then the captain spoke of reading matter, asked advice in regard to suitable books and periodicals, and begged his friends to have a careful oversight of all the mental food of his children.

"You could not entrust that matter to a more wise and capable person than papa," Elsie said, with an affectionate, smiling look at her father. "I well remember how strict he was with me in my childhood. Novels were coveted but forbidden sweets."

"You must have been glad when you were old enough to read them, mamma," remarked Zoe, joining the circle.

"You read far too many, my little woman," said Mr. Dinsmore, pinching her rosy cheek. "If I were Edward, I should curtail the supply and try to cultivate a taste for something better."

"But I'm a married woman and sha'n't submit to being treated like a child, grandpa," she said with a little pout and a toss of her pretty head.

"Not even by me?" asked Edward leaning down over her as he stood behind her chair.

"No, not even by you," she returned saucily, looking up into his face with laughing eyes. "I'm your wife, sir, not your child."

"Both, actually, I should say," laughed Edward. "I remember that I was considered a mere child at your age. And whatever you are, you belong to me, don't you, darling?"

"Yes, and you to me just as much," she retorted, and at that there was a general laugh.

The captain had said nothing of the objectionable reading matter found in his children's hands that day, but when alone with Violet in their own room, he told her all about it. He blamed himself severely for not having been watchful over them as he ought and expressed his distress over the discovery that Max had sometimes been guilty of profanity.

"I do not know whether it has become a habit with him," he said, "but, my dear, I beg you to watch him closely when I am away, and if he is ever known to offend in that way, please see that he is properly punished."

"But how, Levis?" she asked with a troubled look. "I don't know what I can do but talk seriously to him about the wickedness of it."

"I hope you will do that, dear. I have no doubt it would have an excellent effect, for he loves and admires you greatly. But let him be punished by being separated, for at least a week, from the rest of the family, as unworthy to associate with them."

"Oh, that would be very hard, very humiliating for a proud, sensitive, affectionate boy like Max!" she exclaimed. "May we not be more lenient toward him?" and she looked pleadingly into her husband's face.

"No," he said with decision, "but I strongly hope there will be no occasion for such punishment, as he seems sincerely penitent and quite determined not to offend in that way again. I really think my boy wants to do right, but he is a heedless, thoughtless fellow, often going wrong from mere carelessness and forgetfulness. He must be taught to think and to remember."

"I wish he could have his father's constant care and control," sighed Violet.

"I wish he could indeed!" responded the captain. "But principally because I fear he will prove a care and trouble to your grandfather and mother, who, I am inclined to think, are more capable than I of giving him proper training. I shall go away feeling easier in regard to my children's welfare than I ever have before since they lost their mother."

"I am very glad of that, Levis," Violet said, her eyes shining with pleasure, "and I do believe they will have a happy life at Ion."

"It will certainly be their own fault if they do not," he replied.

Rose Travilla was somewhat less amiable in disposition than her mother and older sisters and had been much disgusted with Lulu's exhibition of temper that evening.

Talking with her mother afterward in her dressing room, she said, "Mamma, I wish you hadn't offered to let Lulu Raymond live with us at Ion. I don't at all like the way she behaves, and I wish you and grandpa would tell her father to send her off to boarding school."

"That is rather an unkind wish, Rosie," said her mother. "Perhaps if you had had to endure the same unkind treatment that Lulu has been subjected to since her mother's death, you might have shown as bad a temper as hers. Haven't you at least some pity for the little girl, when you reflect that she is motherless?"

"I don't think she could have a sweeter mother than our Vi," was the unexpected rejoinder. "But she doesn't appreciate her in the least," Rose went on, "but seems always on the watch against any effort on Vi's part to control her."

"She seems to be naturally impatient of control by whomsoever exerted," Mrs. Travilla said. "But we will hope to see her improve in that respect, and you must set her a good example, Rosie.

"And I want you to think how sad it would be for her to be parted from the brother and sister she loves so dearly and sent away alone to boarding school. I shall never forget how alarmed and distressed I was when your grandfather threatened me with one."

"Did he, mamma?" asked Rose, opening her eyes wide with surprise.

"Yes, he was very much displeased with me at the time," her mother said with a sigh. "But we will not talk about it; the recollection of it is very painful to me."

"No, mamma, but I simply cannot get over my astonishment, for I thought you were never naughty, even when you were a little child."

"Quite a mistake, Rosie. I had my naughty times as well as other children," Mrs. Travilla said, smiling at Rosie's bewildered look. "But now I want you to promise me, my child, that you will be kind and forbearing toward poor, motherless Lulu."

"Well, mamma, to please you, I will, but I hope she won't try me too much by impertinence to you or Violet. I don't think I can stand it if she does."

"Try to win her love, Rosie, and then you may be able to influence her strongly for good."

"I don't know how to begin, mamma."

"Force your thoughts to dwell on the good points in her character and think compassionately of the respects in which she is less fortunate than yourself, and you will soon find a feeling of love toward her springing up in your heart—and love begets love. Do her some kindness, daughter, and that will help you to love her and to gain her love."

"Well, mamma, I shall try if only to please you. But do tell me, did grandpa punish you very severely when you were naughty?"

"His punishment was seldom anything more severe than a gentle rebuke—'I am not pleased with you, daughter,' he would say, but I think I felt it more than many a child would a whipping. I did so dearly love my father that nothing was more terrible than his displeasure to me."

"Yes, I know you and he love each other dearly, and he often says you were a very good, extremely conscientious little girl."

"But to return to Lulu," said Mrs. Travilla. "I had thought she would be a nice companion for you, and until this evening I have not seen her show any naughty temper since the first week she was here."

"No, mamma, I guess she actually has been quite well behaved, and perhaps she will prove a pleasant companion. I am sorry for her, too, because she hasn't a dear, wise, kind mother like mine," Rosie added, putting her arms about her mother's neck. "And I am also sorry because her father, who I am sure she loves very much, must soon go away and leave her."

Chapter Fifth

Farewell, God knows when we shall meet again.

—Shakespeare

The next morning the captain and Max were out together on the beach before Violet and the little girls had left their rooms. The lad liked to be alone with his father. He had always been proud and fond of him, and the past few months of constant company had greatly strengthened the bonds of affection between them. The boy's heart was sore at the thought of the parting that must soon come; the captain's hardly less so. He talked very kindly with his son, urging him to make the best use of his time, talents, and opportunities and to grow up to be a good, honorable, and useful man.

"I want to be just such a man as you are, papa," Max said with an admiring, affectionate look up into his father's face as he slipped his own hand into his father's.

The captain clasped the hand lovingly in his and held it fast.

"I trust you will be an even better and more talented man than I, my boy," he said. "But always remember my most ardent wish is to see you a truly good man—a Christian serving God with all your might."

At this moment a voice behind them said, "Good mornin', Cap'n. I'se got a lettah hyah for you, sah."

"Ah, good morning, Ben, and thank you for bringing it," said the captain turning round to receive it.

"You's berry welcome, sah," responded Ben, touching his hat, as he turned away to walk toward Mr. Dinsmore's cottage.

"From Washington," the captain remarked, more to himself than to Max as he broke the seal.

Max watched him while he read, then asked, a little tremulously, "Must you go very soon, papa?"

"Within three days, my dear boy. But we won't say anything about it until after prayers, but let Mamma Vi and your sisters enjoy their breakfast in peace."

"Yes, sir. Papa, I wish I was going with you!"

"But think how your sisters and Mamma Vi would miss you, Max."

"Yes, sir, I suppose they would. I hadn't thought of that."

"Besides, I want you to take my place to Mamma Vi as nearly as you can," added his father, looking smilingly at him.

"Oh, papa, thank you!" cried the boy, his face growing bright with pleased surprise. "I will try my very best and do all for her that I can."

"I don't doubt it, my son. And now let us go in, for it must be breakfast time, I think."

Lulu and Grace ran out to the veranda to meet them with a glad, "Good morning, papa," and held up their faces for a kiss.

It was bestowed heartily as he stooped and gently gathered them into his arms, saying in tender tones, "Good morning, my dear little daughters."

The breakfast bell was ringing, and they hastened to obey its summons. They found Violet already in the dining room looking sweet and fresh as a rose in a pretty, becoming morning dress.

The captain chatted cheerfully with her and the children while he ate, seeming to enjoy his beefsteak, muffins, and coffee. But Max scarcely spoke and occasionally had some difficulty in swallowing his food because of the lump that would rise in his throat at the thought of the parting now drawing so very near.

Directly after breakfast came family worship. Then, as Violet and her husband stood together before the window looking out upon the sea, he gave her his Washington letter to read.

She glanced over it, while he put his arm about her waist.

"Oh, Levis, so soon!" she said tremulously, looking up at him with eyes full of tears, and as her head dropped upon his shoulder, the tears began to fall.

He soothed her with caresses and whispered words of endearment—and of hope, too, that the separation might not be a long one.

"What is it, Max?" whispered Lulu. "Has papa got his orders?"

"Yes, and he has to be off in less than three days," replied Max in husky tones as he hastily brushed away a tear.

Lulu's eyes filled, but by a great effort she kept the tears from falling.

The captain turned toward them. "We are going into the other house, children," he said. "You can come with us if you wish."

"Yes, sir. Thank you, sir," they said. Grace ran to her father and put her tiny hand in his.

They found the Dinsmore and Travilla families assembled in the parlor, discussing plans for the day, all of which were upset by the captain's news.

His ship lay in Boston harbor and it was promptly decided that they would all leave today for that city, only a few hours distant.

As the cottages had been rented furnished and all had for days past held themselves in readiness for sudden departure, this would afford ample time for the necessary packing and other arrangements.

All was presently bustle and activity in both houses. Zoe and Edward, with no painful parting in prospect, made themselves very merry over their packing. They were much like two children and except when overcome by the recollection of her recent bereavement, Zoe was as playful and frolicsome as a kitten.

"Can I help, Mamma Vi?" asked Lulu following Violet into her dressing room.

Vi considered a moment. "You are a dear child to want to help," she said smiling kindly upon the little girl. "I don't think you can pack your trunk, but you can be of use here by handing me things out of the bureau drawers and wardrobe. There are so many trunks to pack that I cannot think of leaving Agnes to do it all."

"My dear," said the captain coming in at that moment, "you are not to do anything but sit in that easy chair and give directions. I flatter myself that I am quite an expert in this line."

"Can you fold ladies' dresses so that they will carry without rumpling?" asked Violet, looking up at him with a saucy smile.

"Perhaps not. I can't say I have ever tried that. Agnes may do that part of the work and I will attend to the rest."

"So, may I hand you the things, papa?" asked Lulu.

"Yes, daughter," he said. "I like to see you trying to be useful."

They set to work, Violet looking on with interest. "Why, you are an excellent packer, Levis," she remarked presently, "far better than I am or Agnes, either, for that matter."

"Thank you," he said. "I am very glad to be able to save you the exertion."

"And you do it so rapidly," she said. "It would have taken me twice as long."

"That is partly because I am stronger and partly the result of a good deal of practice. And Lulu is quite a help," he added with an affectionate look at his daughter.

She flushed with pleasure. "Are you going to pack the other trunks, papa? Max's and Gracie's and mine? And may I help you with them as well?" she asked.

"Yes is my answer to both questions," came his pleasant rejoinder.

"Where are Max and Gracie?" asked Violet.

"I told Max to take his little sister to the beach and take care of and amuse her," the captain said in answer to the question.

"Don't you want to be out at play, too, Lulu?" asked Violet. "I can help your papa."

"No, ma'am, thank you," the child answered in a quick, emphatic way. "I'd much rather be with papa today than playing."

He gave her a pleased look and smile and Violet said, "That is nice, Lulu. I am very glad his children love him so."

"Indeed we do, Mamma Vi, every one of us!" exclaimed Lulu. "Papa knows we do. Don't you, my own dear papa?"

"Yes, I am quite sure of it," he said. "And that my wife is fond of me also," with a smiling glance at her, "and altogether it makes me a very happy man, indeed."

"As you deserve to be," said Violet happily. "Please, sir, will you allow me to fold my dresses?"

"No, for here comes Agnes," as the maid entered the room, "who, I dare say, can do it better. Come, Lulu, we will go now to your room."

Violet stayed where she was to direct and assist Agnes, and Lulu was glad because she wanted to be alone with her father for a while.

When her trunk was packed he turned to leave the room but she detained him. "Papa," she said, clinging to his hand, "I—I want to speak to you."

He sat down and drew her to his side, putting an arm about her waist. "Well, daughter, what is it?" he asked kindly, stroking the hair back from her forehead with his other hand.

"Papa, I—I wanted to tell you that I'm sorry for—for," she stammered, her eyes drooping, her cheeks growing crimson.

"Sorry for your former naughtiness and your rebellion?" he asked gently, as she paused, leaving her sentence unfinished.

"Yes, papa, I couldn't bear to let you go away without telling you so again."

"Well, daughter, it was all forgiven long ago and you have been a pretty good girl most of the time since that first sad week."

"Papa, I do want to be good," she said earnestly, "but somehow the badness will get the better of me."

"Yes, each one of us has an evil nature to fight against," he said. "And it will get the better of us unless we are determined and do battle with it, not in our own strength only, but crying mightily for assistance to Him who has said, 'In Me is thine help.'

"We must watch and pray, my child. The Bible bids us keep our hearts with all diligence and set watch at the door of our lips that we sin not with our tongues. Also, we are to pray without ceasing. We need to cry often to God for help to overcome the evil that is in our own hearts, the snares of the world, and the devil, 'who goeth about as a roaring lion seeking whom he may devour.'"

"Papa," she said, looking up into his face, "do you find it hard to be good sometimes?"

"Yes, my child, I have the same battle to fight that you have, and I am the more sorry for you because I know by experience how difficult it sometimes is to do right."

"And you have to help me by punishing me when I am naughty and making me do as I ought?"

"Yes, and my battle is sometimes for patience with a naughty, disobedient child."

"I think you were very patient with me that time you kept me shut up so long in this room," she said. "If I'd been in your place I'd have taken a good switch and whipped my little girl till I made her obey me at once."

"Do you think that would have been the better plan, Lulu?"

"No, sir. I think you'd have had to 'most kill me before I'd have given up, but if I'd been in your place I wouldn't have had the patience to wait."

"You need to cultivate the grace of patience, then," he said gravely. "Now come with me to Max's room, and let us see if we can pack up his goods and belongings."

"Papa, I almost think I could pack it myself after watching you pack all these others."

"Possibly, but I shall do it more quickly with you to help in getting all the things together."

Everyone was ready in due season for departure, and that night the two cottages that for months past had been so full of light and life were dark, silent, and deserted.

Arriving in Boston, the whole party took rooms at one of the principal hotels. There they spent the night, but the greater part of the next day was passed on board the captain's vessel.

The day of parting came all too quickly—a very hard one for him, his young wife, and children. Little, feeble Gracie cried herself sick, and Violet found it necessary to put aside the indulgence of her own grief in order to comfort the nearly heartbroken child, who clung to her as she might have done to her own mother.

Max and Lulu made no loud lament, but their quiet, subdued manner and sad countenances told of deep and sincere sorrow. And in truth, they often felt ready to join in Gracie's oft-repeated cry, "Oh, how can I do without my dear, dear papa again?"

But they were with kind friends. Everyone in the party showed them sympathy. Pretty presents were made for them and they were taken to see all the sights of the city likely to interest them.

Grandma Elsie particularly endeared herself to them at this time by her motherly tenderness and care, treating them as if they were her own children.

Their father had given each two parting gifts—a handsome pocket Bible with the injunction to commit at least one verse to memory every day and a pretty purse with some spending money in it. He knew they would enjoy making purchases for themselves when visiting the city stores with the older people.

So they did. Lulu, who was generous to a fault, had soon spent all of hers on gifts for others—a new doll for Gracie, some books for Max, a bottle of perfume for Mamma Vi, and a toy for Walter.

Violet was much pleased with the present from Lulu as an evidence of growing affection. She received it with warm thanks and a loving embrace. "My dear child, it is very kind of you to think of me!" she said. "It makes me hope you have really given me a little place in your heart, dear."

"Oh, yes, Mamma Vi, indeed I have!" cried the little girl, returning the embrace. "Surely we ought all to love you when you love our dear father so much, and he loves you, too."

"Certainly," said Max, who was standing by, "we couldn't help loving so sweet and pretty a lady if she was nothing at all to us and we lived in the same house with her. How could we think any less, especially when she's married to our father?"

"And how can I help loving you because you are the children of my dear husband?" responded Violet, taking the boy's hand and pressing it warmly in hers.

Some hours later Violet accidentally overheard part of a conversation between her little sister Rose and Lulu.

"Yes," Rosie was saying, "mamma gives me fifty cents a week for spending money,"

"Ah, how nice!" exclaimed Lulu. "Papa often gives us some money, but not regularly, and Max and I have often talked together about how much we would like to have a regular allowance. I'd be delighted even if it wasn't more than ten cents."

Violet had been wishing to give the children something and trying to find out what would be most acceptable. So, she was greatly pleased with the hint given her by this little speech of Lulu's.

The child came presently to her side to bid her good night. Violet put an arm around her and kissing her affectionately said, "Lulu, I have been thinking you might like to have an allowance of pocket money, as Rosie has. Would you?"

"Oh, Mamma Vi! I'd like it better than anything else I can think of!" cried the little girl, her face sparkling with delight.

"Then you shall have it and begin now," Violet said while taking out her purse and putting two bright silver quarters into Lulu's hand.

"Oh, thank you, mamma, how good and kind of you!" cried the child.

"Max shall have the same," said Violet, "and Gracie half as much for the present. When she is a little older it shall be doubled. Would you like the pleasure of telling Max and taking this to him?" she asked, putting a half dollar into Lulu's hand.

"Oh, yes, ma'am! Thank you very much!"

Max was on the far side of the room, a parlor of good size in the hotel where they were staying, and he seemed very much absorbed in a storybook. Lulu approached him softly, a gleeful smile on her lips and in her eyes, and laid his half dollar on the open page.

"What's that for?" he asked, looking round at her.

"For you. And you're to have as much every week, Mamma Vi says."

"Oh, Lu, am I, really?"

"Yes, I, too, and Gracie's to have a quarter."

"Oh, isn't it splendid!" he cried and hurried to Violet to pour out his thanks.

Grandma Elsie, seated on the sofa by Violet's side, shared with her the pleasure of witnessing the children's delight.

The party had now spent several days in Boston. The next morning they left for Philadelphia, where they were to pay a short visit to the Allisons as their last halt on the journey home to Ion.

Chapter Sixth

To the guiltless heart, where'er we roam,
No scenes delight us like our much-loved home.

Elsie and her children had greatly enjoyed their summer up north, but now were filled with content and happiness at the thought of soon seeing again their loved home at Ion. Max and Lulu looked forward with pleasing anticipations and eager curiosity to their first sight of it, having heard various glowing descriptions of it from Mamma Vi and Rosie.

Their father, too, had spoken of it as a home so delightful that they ought to feel the liveliest gratitude for having been invited to share its blessings.

It looked very beautiful, very inviting, upon the arrival of the travelers late in the afternoon of a warm, bright October day.

The woods and the trees that bordered the avenue were in the height of their autumnal glory, the gardens bright with many flowers of the most varied and brilliant hues, and the lengthening shadows slept on a still green and velvety lawn.

As their carriage turned into the avenue, Elsie bent an affectionate, smiling look upon Max and Lulu, and taking a hand of each, said in sweetest tones, "Welcome to your new home, my dears, and may it prove to you a very, very happy one."

"Thank you ma'am," they both responded, Max adding, "I am very glad, Grandma Elsie, that I am to live with you and Mamma Vi."

"I, too," said Lulu, "and in such a pretty place. Oh, how lovely everything does look!"

The air was delightful and doors and windows stood wide open. On the veranda a welcoming group had gathered. Elsie's brother and sister—Horace Dinsmore, Jr., of the Oaks and Mrs. Rose Lacey from the Laurels—and her cousins Calhoun and Arthur Conly were there. While a little in the rear of them were the servants, all—from old Uncle Joe, now in his ninety-fifth year, down to Betty, his ten-year-old great-granddaughter—showing faces full of eager delight.

They stood back respectfully till greetings had been exchanged between relatives and friends, then pressed forward with their words of welcome, sure of a shake of the hand and a kind word from each member of the family.

Mr. Dinsmore held little Gracie in his arms. She was much fatigued and exhausted by the long journey.

"Here is a patient for you, Arthur," he said, "and I am very glad you are here to attend to her."

"Yes," said Violet, "her father charged me to put her in your care."

"Then let her be put immediately to bed," said Arthur after a moment's scrutiny of the child. "Give her to me, uncle, and I will carry her upstairs."

"To my room," added Violet.

But the child shrank from the stranger and clung to Mr. Dinsmore.

"No, thank you, I will take her up myself," he said. "I am fully equal to it," and he moved on through the hall and up the broad stairway, Violet and the doctor following.

The others presently scattered to their rooms to rid themselves of the dust of travel and to dress for the evening.

"Well, little wife, is it nice to be at home again?" Edward asked with a smiling look at Zoe as they entered their apartments.

"Yes, indeed!" she cried, sending a swift glance around the neat and tastefully furnished room, "especially such a home and to be shared with such nice people—one in particular who shall for now be nameless," she added with an arch look and smile.

"One who hopes you will never tire of his company as he never expects to of yours," returned Edward catching her in his arms and snatching a kiss from her full, red lips.

"Now, don't," she said, pushing him away. "Just wait till I've washed the dust from my face. Here come our trunks," as two of the men servants brought them in, "and you must tell me what dress to put on."

"You look so lovely in any and every one of the dozen or more that I have small choice in the matter," laughed the young husband.

"What gross flattery!" she exclaimed. "Well, then, I suppose I'll have to choose for myself. But you mustn't complain if I do that some time when you don't want me to."

The two Elsies had lingered a little behind the others due to the fact that the older servants had so many words of welcome to say to them—the younger one especially—because she had been so far and so long away.

And the babe had to be handed about from one to another, kissed and blessed and remarked upon as to his real or fancied resemblance to this or that older member of the family.

"It do 'pear pow'ful strange, Miss Elsie, dat you went away young lady and come back wid husband and baby," remarked Aunt Dicey. "And it don't seem but yistiday dat you was a little bit ob a gal yoself."

"Yes, I have come back a great deal richer than I went," Elsie returned, with a glance of mingled love and joy, first at her husband, then at her infant son. "I have great reason to be thankful."

At that moment Mrs. Travilla became aware that Max and Lulu were lingering near, as if not knowing quite what to do with themselves.

"Ah, my dears," she said, turning to them with a kind and pleasant look, "has no one attended to you? Come with me and I will show you directly to your rooms."

They followed her up the stairs and each was shown into a pleasant room tastefully furnished and with every comfort and convenience.

Lulu's had two doors, one opening into the hall, the other into her mamma's bedroom.

Elsie explained this, adding, "So if you are in want of anything or should feel frightened or lonely in the night, you can run right into the room where you will find your mamma and Gracie."

"Yes, ma'am, that is very nice; and oh, what a pretty room! How kind and good you are to me and to my brother and sister, too!" cried Lulu, her eyes shining with gratitude and pleasure.

"I am very glad to be able to do it," Elsie said, taking the little girl's hand in one of hers and smoothing her hair caressingly with the other—for Lulu had taken off her hat. "I want to be like a mother to you, dear child, and to your brother and sister since my daughter is too young for so great care and responsibility. I love you all, and want you to come freely to me with your troubles and perplexities, your joys and sorrows, just as my own children have done. I want you to feel that you have a right to do so because I have invited you."

She bent down and kissed Lulu's lips and the little girl threw her arms about her neck with impulsive warmth, saying, "Dear Grandma Elsie, I love you and thank you ever so much! And I mean to try ever so hard to be good," she added with a blush, hanging her head shamefacedly. "I know I'm often very naughty; papa said I give him more anxiety than Max and Gracie both put together. I'm afraid I can't be good all the time, but I do mean to try hard."

"Well, dear, if you try with all your might, asking help from on high, you will succeed at last," Elsie said. "And now I will leave you to wash and dress. I see your trunk has been brought up and opened, so that you should have no difficulty."

With that Elsie passed on into Violet's rooms to see how Gracie was. She found her sleeping sweetly in Violet's bed, the latter bending over her with a very tender, motherly look on her fair, young face.

"Is she not a darling, mamma?" she whispered softly, turning her head at the sound of her mother's light footstep.

"She is a very engaging child," replied Elsie. "I think we are all fond of her, but you especially."

"Yes, mamma, I love her for herself, her gentle, affectionate disposition, but still more because she is my husband's child—his dear baby girl, as he so often calls her."

"Ah, I understand that," Elsie said, with a loving, though rather sad look and smile into Violet's azure eyes, "for I have often felt just so in regard to my own children. What does Arthur say about her?"

"That she is more in need of rest and sleep than anything else at present. He will see her again tomorrow and will probably be able then to give me full directions in regard to her diet and so forth."

"You will come down to supper? You will not think it necessary to stay with her yourself?" Elsie said inquiringly.

"Oh, no, mamma! I shall dress at once. I should not like to miss being with you all," Violet answered, moving away from the bedside. "Ah!" with sudden recollection, "I have been quite forgetting both Max and Lulu."

"I have seen them to their rooms," her mother said, "and now I must go and attend to Rosie and Walter and to my own grooming."

"Dear mamma, thank you!" Violet said heartily.

"My dear, I consider them quite as much my children, and therefore my special charge, as yours, perhaps a trifle more," Elsie returned with sprightly look and tone as she left the room.

Agnes was in attendance on her young mistress and was presently sent to ask if Lulu was in need of help, and to say that her mamma would like to see her before she went downstairs.

"I don't need anything till I'm ready to have my sash tied," answered Lulu, "and then I'll come in to Mamma Vi and you to have it done. She was very good to send you, Agnes, and you to come."

"La! Chile, it's jus' my business to mind Miss Wilet," returned Agnes. "An' she's good to eberybody, ob cose—always was."

"What would you like to see me for, Mamma Vi?" asked Lulu as she entered her young stepmother's dressing room.

"Just to make sure that your hair and dress are all right, dear. You know we have company tonight, and I am particularly anxious that my little Lulu shall look her very best."

The child's face flushed with pleasure. She liked to be well and becomingly dressed, and it was gratifying to have Mamma Vi care that she should be. Mrs. Scrimp was so different. She had never cared whether Lulu's attire was tasteful and becoming or quite the reverse but always roused the child's indignation by telling her it was sufficient if she were only neat and clean.

"Am I all right?" she asked, twirling around.

"Pretty nearly. We will have you quite so in a minute," Violet answered. "Tie her sash, Agnes, and smooth down the folds of her dress, please."

"Mamma Vi, is that strange lady any relation to you?" asked Lulu.

"Yes, she is my aunt, mamma's sister."

"She is quite pretty, but not nearly so pretty as Grandma Elsie."

"No, I have always thought no one else could be half so beautiful as mamma."

"Why, Mamma Vi, you are yourself!" exclaimed Lulu in a tone of honest sincerity that made Violet laugh out loud.

"That is just your own notion, little girl," she said, giving the child a kiss.

"Oh, I have eyes and can see! Besides, papa thinks so, too, and Max and Gracie."

"Yes, my dear husband! He loves me and love is blind," murmured Vi, half to herself, with a sigh and a far off look in the lovely azure eyes. Her thoughts were following him over the deep, wide, treacherous sea.

She stole on tiptoe into the next room for another peek at his sleeping baby girl, Lulu going with her. Then, hearing the tea bell, they went down to the dining room together.

They gathered about the table, a large cheerful party—the travelers full of satisfaction at being home again, the others so glad to have them there once more.

Zoe was very merry and Rosie in almost wild spirits, but Max and Lulu, to whom all was new and strange, were quite quiet and subdued, scarcely speaking except when spoken to. "Mamma," Rosie said when they had adjourned to the parlor, "it's lovely out of doors—bright moonlight and not a bit cold. Mayn't I take Max and Lulu down to our little lakelet?"

"Do you think the evening air would be injurious to them, Arthur?" Mrs. Travilla asked, turning to her cousin.

"I think there may be malaria in it and would advise them to stay within doors until after breakfast tomorrow morning," he answered, drawing Rosie to a seat on his knee.

"Then you'd better let us go," she said archly, "so you can have some more patients. Don't you like to have plenty of patients?"

"That's a leading question, little cuz," he said laughingly, toying with her curls. "When people are sick, I like to have an opportunity to exercise my skill in trying to relieve and cure them, but I hope I don't want them sick in order to furnish me with certain employment."

"I want to show Lulu and Max the beauties of Ion, and I don't know how I could possibly wait till tomorrow," she said.

"Then take them about from one room to another and let them look out through the windows upon its moonlit lawn, alleys, gardens, and the lakelet."

"Oh, yes, yes! That will do!" she cried, leaving his knee in haste to carry out his suggestion.

Max and Lulu accepted her invitation, and they ran in and out, upstairs and down, the young strangers delighted with the views thus obtained of their new home and its surroundings.

Rosie said she hoped they would not be required to begin lessons immediately but would be allowed a few days in which to enjoy walks, rides, drives, and boating.

"I'll ask grandpa and mamma if we may," she added as they re-entered the parlor. She hastened to present her petition, and it was granted. The children were told they should have a week in which to enjoy themselves and recover from the fatigue of their journey and would be expected to show their appreciation of the indulgence by great level of industry afterward.

Lulu was standing a little apart from the rest, gazing out of a window upon the moonlit lawn, when a step drew near. Then, someone took her by the arm and in a twinkling she found herself seated upon a gentleman's knee.

"Well, my little, dark-eyed lassie," he said, "no one has thought it worth while to introduce us, but we won't let that hinder our making acquaintance. Do you know who I am?"

"I heard Rosie call you Uncle Horace."

"Then suppose you follow Rosie's example. If you are as good as you are bonny, I shall be proud to claim you as my niece."

"But I'm not," she said frankly. Then quite hastily correcting herself, continued, "I don't mean to say I'm not bonny, but I'm not good. Aunt Beulah used to say I was the worst child she ever saw."

"Indeed! You are honest, at all events," he said with a look of amusement. "And who, may I ask, is Aunt Beulah?"

"The person Gracie and I lived with before papa got married to Mamma Vi."

"Ah! Well, I shall not regard her opinion, but wait and form one for myself. I shall certainly be much surprised if you don't turn out a pattern good girl, now that you are to live with my sweet sister, Elsie. In the meantime, my dear, will it please you to call me Uncle Horace?"

"Yes, sir, since you asked me to," Lulu replied looking much gratified.

At this moment the door opened and Mr. Lacey walked in. He had come for his wife, and when he and the others had exchanged greetings, she rose to make ready for departure.

Calhoun Conly rose also, saying to his brother, "Well, Art, perhaps it would be as well for us to go, too. Our friends must be tired after their long journey and will want to get to bed early."

"Suppose you all delay a little and unite with us in evening family worship," said Mr. Dinsmore. "It has been a good while since I have had all three of my children present with me at such a service."

All complied with his request and immediately afterward took leave. Then with an exchange of affectionate good nights, the family separated and scattered to their rooms.

Lulu was not quite ready for bed when Violet came in. Putting her arm around her, she asked with a gentle kiss, "Do you feel strange and lonely in this new place, little girl?"

"Oh, no, Mamma Vi! It seems such a nice home that I am very glad to be in it."

"That is right," Violet said, repeating her caress. "I hope you will sleep well and wake refreshed. I shall leave the door open between your room and mine so that you need not feel timid. You can run right in to me whenever you wish. Good night, my dear."

"Good night, Mamma Vi. Thank you for being so good to me, and to Gracie and Max," Lulu said, clinging to her in an affectionate way.

"My child," returned Violet, "how could I be anything else to the children of my dear husband? Ah, I must go! Mamma calls me," she added, hurrying away as a soft, sweet voice was heard coming from the adjoining room.

Lulu finished undressing, said her prayers, and had just laid her head on her pillow, when someone glided noiselessly to her bedside and passed a soft hand caressingly over her hair.

The child opened her eyes, which had already half closed in sleep, and saw by the moonlight a sweet and beautiful face bending lovingly over her.

"Grandma Elsie," she murmured sleepily.

"Yes, dear. Rosie and Walter never like to go to sleep without a good-night kiss from their mamma, and you must have the same now, as you are to be as one of my dear children."

Lulu, now wide awake again, started up to put both arms around the neck of her visitor. "Oh, I do love you!" she said. "And I'll try hard to be a good child to you."

"I believe it, dear," Elsie said, pressing the child to her heart. "Will you join my children in their half hour with mamma in her dressing room before breakfast? I shall be glad to have you, but you must do just as you please about it."

"Thank you, ma'am, I'll come," said Lulu.

"That is right. Now lie down and go to sleep. You need a long night's rest."

Chapter Seventh

Her fancy follow'd him through foaming waves
To distant shores.

—Cowper

Violet, in her nightdress with her beautiful hair unbound and hanging about her like a golden cloud, stood before her dressing table, gazing through a mist of unshed tears upon a miniature that she held in her hand.

"Ah, where are you now, my love?" she sighed half aloud.

Her mother's voice answered close at her side, in gentle, tender accents, "In God's keeping, my darling. He is the God of the sea as well as of the land."

"Yes, mamma, and his God as well as mine," Violet responded, looking up and smiling through her tears. "Ah, what comfort in both assurances and in the precious promise, 'Behold, I am with thee, and will keep thee in all places, whither thou goest.' It is his and it is mine."

"Yes, dearest. I feel for you in your loneliness," her mother said, putting her arms around her. "Elsie is very happy in her husband and baby, Edward in his wife. They need me but little, comparatively, but you and I must draw close together and be a comfort and support to each other. Shall we not do so, my love?"

"Yes, indeed, dearest mamma. Oh, what a great comfort and blessing you are to me, and you always have been! And I am happier and less lonely for having my husband's children with me, especially my darling little Gracie. I feel that in caring for her and nursing her back to health I shall be adding to his happiness."

"As no doubt you will," her mother said. "It will be a pleasure to me to help you care for her and the others, also. Now, good night, daughter, we both ought to be in bed."

Violet presently stretched herself beside the sleeping Gracie. With a softly murmured word of endearment, she drew the child closer to her and in another moment shared her slumbers.

When she awoke the sun was shining, and the first object her eyes rested upon was the little face by her side. The pallor and look of exhaustion it had worn the night before were quite gone—a faint tinge of pink had even stolen into her cheeks.

Violet noted the change with a feeling of relief and thankfulness to God. Raising herself upon an elbow, she touched her lips lightly to the soft and white forehead.

The child's eyes flew open and with a sweet, engaging smile she asked, "Have you been lying beside me all night, mamma?"

"Yes, Gracie. You have had a long sleep, dear. Do you feel quite rested?"

"Yes, mamma, I feel very well. This is such a nice soft bed, and I like to sleep with you. May I always do so?"

"For all winter, I think, dear. I like to have your papa's baby girl by my side."

"I'm very much obliged to him for finding me such a sweet, pretty, new mamma. I told him so one day," remarked the child innocently, putting her arm about Vi's neck.

"Did you?" Violet asked with an amused smile. "And what did he say?"

"Nothing, he just smiled and hugged me tight and kissed me ever so many times. Do you know what made him do that, mamma?"

"Because he likes to have us love one another. And so we will, won't we dear?"

"Yes, indeed! Mamma, I feel a little hungry."

"I'm glad to hear it, for here comes Agnes with a glass of nice, rich milk for you. And when you have drunk it she will wash and dress you. We will all have to hurry a little to be ready in good time for breakfast," she added, springing from the bed and beginning to get dressed. "Grandpa Dinsmore does not like to have us late."

"Miss Rosie and Miss Lulu's up and dressed and gone into Miss Elsie's room, Miss Wilet," remarked Agnes, holding the tumbler she had brought to Gracie's lips.

"Ah, that is well," said Violet, with a pleased look. "Lulu has stolen a march on us, Gracie."

The week that followed their arrival at Ion was a delightful one to all, especially the children, who had scarce anything to do but enjoy themselves. The weather was all that could be desired, and they walked, rode, drove, boated, fished, and went nutting.

Mr. Dinsmore and Edward were every day more or less busied with the affairs of the plantation, but someone of the older people could always find time to be with the children, while Zoe never failed to make one of the party. She seemed almost as much a child as any of the younger ones.

Every nook and cranny of the plantation and its neighborhood was explored. Visits were paid to Fairview, the Laurels, the Pines, the Oaks, Roselands, and Ashlands—the dwellers at each place having first called upon the family at Ion.

Both Max and Lulu had long desired to learn to ride on horseback, and great was their delight on learning that now this wish could be gratified.

A pony was always at the service of each, and lessons in the art of sitting and managing it were given them. Some were given by Mr. Dinsmore and some by Edward, who was a great admirer of his brother-in-law, Captain Raymond, and had become much attached to him. He, therefore, had also a very kindly interest in his children.

Gracie was given a share in all the pleasures for which she was considered strong enough. When she was not able to go with the others on their expeditions, she was well-entertained at home with toys and books filled with pictures and stories suited to her age.

Both Elsie and Violet watched over the little girl with true motherly love and care. She warmly returned the affection of both, but clung especially to Violet, her "pretty new mamma."

Gracie was a docile, little creature and seemed very happy in her new life. She was deeply interested in the riding lessons of her brother and sister. So, when, near the end of the week, Dr. Arthur, to whom she was becoming much attached, set her on the back of a Shetland pony and led it about the grounds for a few minutes, promising her longer rides as her strength increased, she was almost speechless with happiness.

With the second week, lessons began in earnest for the children. Each task had its appointed hour. They were required to be as systematic, punctual, and well-prepared for recitations as pupils in an ordinary school. But, at the same time, great care was taken that neither mind nor body should be overtaxed. They enjoyed many liberties and indulgences that could not have been granted elsewhere than at home.

The mornings were spent by Rosie and Lulu in the schoolroom in both study and recitation under the supervision of either Grandma Elsie or Mamma Vi.

Grace and Walter would be there also at the start, but their short and easy tasks having been attended to, they might stay and amuse themselves quietly, or if inclined for noisy sport, go to the nursery or playroom to enjoy it there.

Max studied his lessons alone in his own room, joining the others when the hour arrived for reciting to Mr. Dinsmore, who took sole charge of his education. He also took charge of the two little girls so far as Latin and arithmetic were concerned. Rosie and Max were together in both these studies. But Lulu—because of being younger and not so far advanced—was alone in both, much to her dissatisfaction, for she was by no means desirous to have Mr. Dinsmore's total attention concentrated upon herself for even a short space of time.

His keen, dark eyes seemed to look her through and through, and though he had never shown her any sternness, she was quite sure he could and would if she gave him any occasion.

But for that there was no necessity, his requirements being always reasonable and only such as she was fully capable of meeting. She had a good mind, quick discernment, and retentive memory, and she was quite resolved to be industrious and to keep her promise to her father to be a good girl in every way. Also, her ambition was aroused to attempt to overtake her brother and Rosie.

She was moderately fond of study, but had a decided repugnance to plain sewing. Therefore, she looked ill-pleased enough upon discovering that it was to be numbered among her daily tasks.

"I hate sewing!" she said with a scowl to no one in particular. "And when I'm old enough to do as I please, I'll never touch a needle and thread."

It was the afternoon of their first school day and the little girls had just repaired to the schoolroom in obedience to directions given them upon their dismissal for the morning.

All the ladies of the family were there, gathered cozily about the fire and the table at which Grandma Elsie was busily cutting out garments that seemed to be intended for a child. But the materials seemed of a coarser, heavier weight than any of the family were accustomed to wearing.

"Perhaps you may change your mind by that time," Grandma Elsie answered Lulu with pleasant tone and smile, "and I hope you will find it more agreeable now than you expect. You are a kind-hearted little girl, I know, and when I tell you these clothes are for a little Indian girl who needs them sadly, I am quite sure you will be glad to help in making them."

Lulu's brow cleared. "Yes, ma'am," she said with a little hesitation, "if I could sew nicely, but I can't."

"The more you need to learn then, dear. Mamma Vi is basting a seam for you and will show you how to sew it."

"And when we all get started there'll be some nice story read aloud, won't there, mamma?" asked Rosie.

"Yes, your sister Elsie will be the reader today and the book Scott's *Lady of the Lake*."

"Oh, how very nice, indeed!" cried Rosie in delight. "It's such a lovely book, and sister Elsie's such a beautiful reader."

"In my little sister's opinion," laughed Mrs. Leland.

"And that of all present, I presume," said Grandma Rose.

"I am fortunate in having so appreciative and loving an audience," returned Elsie merrily.

Lulu had accepted a mute invitation to take a seat by Violet's side.

"Mamma Vi," she whispered with heightened color, "I can't sew as well as Gracie and I'm ashamed to have anybody see my poor work."

"Never mind, dear, we won't show your first attempts, and you will find this coarse, soft muslin easy to learn on," Violet answered in the same low tone. "See, this is the way," taking a few stitches. "Your father told me he wanted his dear little girls to learn every womanly accomplishment, and I feel sure you will do your best to please him. Take pains and you may be able to send him a sample of your work as a Christmas gift. Now, tell me, would you not enjoy that, Lulu?"

"Yes, ma'am. Yes, indeed!" returned the little girl, setting resolutely to work.

"Mamma," said Gracie, coming to Violet's other side, "mayn't I have some work, too? I like sewing better than Lulu does. Aunt Beulah taught me to overseam and to hem."

"Then you may help us, little girlie," Violet said, kissing the little, fair cheek, "but must stop the minute you begin to feel fatigued—for I must not let papa's baby girl wear out her small strength."

Presently, all having been supplied with work, the reading began. Everyone seemed able to listen with enjoyment except Lulu, who bent over her task with frowning face, making her needle go in and out with impatient pushes and jerks.

Violet watched the performance furtively for a few minutes, then gently taking the work from her, said in a pleasant undertone, "You are getting your stitches too long and too far apart, dear. We will take them out, and you shall try again."

"I can't do it right! I'll never succeed, if I try ever so hard!" muttered Lulu impatiently.

"Oh, yes, you will," returned Violet with an encouraging smile. "Keep trying, and you will be surprised to find how easy it will grow."

The second attempt was quite an improvement upon the first, and under Violet's pleased look and warm praises Lulu's ruffled temper smoothed down and the ugly frown left her face.

In the meanwhile, Gracie was handling her own needle with the quiet ease of one accustomed to its use, making tiny, even stitches that quite surprised her new mamma.

With all her faults, Lulu was incapable of envy or jealousy, especially toward her dearly loved brother and sister, and when at the close of the sewing hour, Gracie's work was handed about from one to another, receiving hearty commendation, no one was better pleased than Lulu.

"Isn't it nice, Grandma Elsie?" she said, glancing at her little sister with a flush of pride in her skill. "A great deal better than I can do, though she's two years younger."

"It's only because I couldn't run about and play like Lulu, and so I just sat beside Aunt Beulah and learned to hem and back stitch and run and overseam," said Gracie. "But Lulu can do everything else better than I can."

"And she will soon equal you in that, I trust," said Violet, with an affectionate glance from one to the other. "I am quite sure she will if she continues to try as she has done today. And it truly makes my heart rejoice to see how much you love one another, dear children."

"I think everybody loves Gracie, because she's hardly ever naughty," said Lulu. "I wish I'd been made so."

Chapter Eighth

Where'er I roam, whatever realms to see,
My heart untraveled fondly turns to thee.

—GOLDSMITH

"How very pretty, Zoe!" said Violet, as she examined her young sister-in-law's work—a piece of fine, black satin upon which she was embroidering large leaves and flowers in the brightest-colored silks.

"Oh, isn't it!" cried Lulu in delighted admiration. "Mamma Vi, I'd like to learn that kind of sewing."

"So you shall, dear, someday, but mamma's theory is that plain sewing should be thoroughly mastered first. That has been her plan with all her children, and Rosie has done scarcely any fancy work, yet."

"But mamma has promised to let me learn all I can about it this winter," remarked Rosie with much satisfaction.

"Mamma," Zoe said with a blush, "I'm afraid I ought to join your plain sewing class. I should be really ashamed to exhibit any of my work in that plain line."

"Well, dear child, I shall be glad to receive you as a pupil if you desire it," Elsie returned, giving her a motherly glance and smile.

"Hark!" exclaimed Zoe, hastily gathering up her work, her cheeks rosy and eyes sparkling with pleasure. "I hear Edward's step and voice," and she tripped out of the room.

"How fond she is of him!" Violet remarked, looking after her with a pleased smile.

"Yes," said her mother, "it does my heart good to see how they love each other. And I think we are all growing fond of Zoe."

"Yes, indeed, mamma!" came in chorus from her three daughters.

"I'm sure we are—my husband and I as well as the rest," added Mrs. Dinsmore.

"And, Vi," said Elsie Leland laughingly, "I really think mamma's new sons are as highly appreciated in the family as her new daughter, and that all three new children dote upon their new mother. Mamma, Lester says you are a pattern mother-in-law, and I answer, 'Of course, mamma is a pattern in every relation in life.'"

"My child, please don't allow yourself to become a flatterer," returned her mother gravely.

"Zoe, Zoe, where are you?" Edward was calling from below.

"Here," she answered, running down to meet him. "I've been in the schoolroom with mamma and the others," she added as she gained his side, looking up brightly into his face as she spoke.

"Ah," he said bending down to kiss the ruby lips, "I thought you were to be my pupil."

"So I am, except in feminine accomplishments. See!" holding up her work. "I've been busy with this. It was the sewing hour and sister Elsie read aloud to us while we worked."

"Ah, yes, I have been reader many a time while mamma and sisters plied the needle."

"How nice! You are such a good reader! But she is almost as good."

"Not only almost, but altogether," he returned merrily as he held open the door of her boudoir for her to enter, then followed her in. "I've come now to hear your recitations. I suppose you are quite prepared," he added, drawing up a chair for her and glancing at a pile of books laying on the table.

"No," she said, coloring and dropping her eye with a slightly mortified air. "I meant to be, but so many things happened to interfere. I had a letter to write, then some ladies called, and then—"

"Well?" he said interrogatively, as she paused, coloring still more deeply.

"I wanted to finish the book I was reading last night. I really couldn't fix my thoughts on stupid lessons until I knew what had become of the heroine."

Edward stood by her side and looked down at her, shaking his head gravely. "It is my belief that duties should be attended to first, Zoe, pleasures indulged in afterward."

"You are talking down to me as if I were nothing but a child!" she cried indignantly, her cheeks growing hot and red.

"The dearest, most lovable child in the world," he said, bending down to stroke her hair and look into her face with laughing eyes.

"No, sir, I am your wife. What did you marry me for if you considered me such a child?" she cried with a pout on her lip, but love-light in the eyes lifted to his.

"Because I loved you and wanted the right to take care of you, my bonny belle," he said, repeating his fond caress.

"And you do, the best care in the world, you dear boy!" she exclaimed impulsively, throwing her arms around his neck. "And if it will please you, I'll set to work on the lessons now."

"Then do, love. I have letters to write and we will sit here and work side by side."

Both worked diligently for an hour or more. They had a merry time over the recitations, then drove together to the nearest village to post Edward's letters and get the afternoon mail for Ion.

Violet was made happy by a long letter from her distant husband.

She barely had time to glance over it, learning when and where it was written, and that he was well at the time of writing, when the tea bell rang.

She slipped the precious missive into her pocket with a little sigh of satisfaction and joined the others at the table with a very bright and happy face.

She had not been the only fortunate one. Her mother had cheering news from Herbert and Harold. Mrs. Dinsmore had some sprightly, gossipy letters from her sisters, Adelaide and May. The contents of the latter furnished topics of lively discussion, in which Violet took part.

She had not mentioned her own letter, but at length Edward, noting the extreme brightness of her countenance, asked, "Is it good news from the captain, then, Vi?"

"Yes, thank you," she said. "He was well and seemingly in good spirits at the time of writing, though he says he misses wife and children sorely."

All three of his children turned toward her with eager, questioning looks, and Max and Lulu asked togather, "Didn't papa write to us, too?"

"He sends you a message, dears," Violet said. "I have not really read the letter yet, but shall do so after supper. You shall all surely have your fair share of it."

On leaving the table they followed her to the door of her boudoir.

"May we come in, Mamma Vi?" Max asked with a wistful look.

"Certainly," she answered in a pleasant tone, though longing to be quite alone while giving her precious letter its first perusal. "I would have you feel free to come into my apartments as I always have felt to go into my mamma's. Sit down and make yourselves comfortable, dears, and you shall hear presently what your papa says.

"The letter was written on shipboard, brought into New York by another vessel, and there mailed to me."

Max politely drew up a chair near the light for Violet, another for Lulu, and placed Gracie's own little rocker close to her mamma's side. He then stood behind Gracie prepared to give close attention to the reading of his father's letter.

Violet omitted a little here and there—tender expressions of affection for herself, or something else evidently intended for her eye alone. The captain wrote delightful letters—at least they were such in the esteem of his wife and children. This one provoked both laughter and tears. He had so amusing a way of relating trivial incidents, while some passages were so tenderly affectionate.

But something near the close brought an anxious, troubled look to Max's face, a frown to Lulu's brow.

It was this: "Tell Max and Lulu I wish each of them to keep a diary for my inspection, writing down every evening what have been the doings and happenings of the day as regards themselves—their studies, their pleasures, their conduct also. Max telling of himself, Lulu of herself, just as they would if sitting on my knee and answering the questions, 'What have you been busy about today? Have you been attentive to your studies, respectful and obedient to those in charge of you? Have you tried to do your duty toward God and man?'

"They need not show anyone at Ion what they write. I shall trust to their truthfulness and honesty not to represent themselves as better than they are, not to hide their faults from the father who cares to know them, only that he may help his dear children to live right and happy. Ah, if they knew how I love them! And how it grieves and troubles me when they go astray!"

Max's face brightened at those closing sentences. Lulu's softened for a moment, but then, as Violet folded the letter, she burst out, "I don't want to! Why does papa say we must do such things?"

"He tells you, dear. Did you not notice?" said Violet. "He says he wishes to know your faults in order to help you correct them. And don't you think it will help you to avoid wrongdoing? To resist temptation? The remembrance that it must be confessed to your dear father and that it will grieve him very much? Is it not kind of him to be willing to bear that pain for the sake of doing you good?"

Lulu did not answer, but Max said, "Yes, indeed, Mamma Vi! And, oh, I hope I'll never have to make his heart ache over my wrongdoings! But I don't know how to keep a diary."

"Nor I, either," added Lulu.

"But you can learn, dears," Violet said. "I will help you at the start. You can each give a very good report of today's conduct, I am sure.

"The keeping of the diary will also help you in a literary way, teaching you to express your thoughts readily in writing. And that, I presume, is one thing your father has in mind."

"But it will be just like writing compositions, and that I always did hate!" cried Lulu vehemently.

"No, not exactly," said Max, "because you don't have to make up anything, only to tell real happenings and doings that you haven't had time to forget."

"And I think you will soon find it making the writing of compositions easier, as well," remarked Violet with an encouraging smile.

"It'll be the same as having to write a composition every day," grumbled Lulu. "I wish papa wouldn't be so hard on us. I have to study lessons a whole hour every evening; and then it'll take ever so long to write; and I shall not have a bit of time to play."

"I wish I could write," Gracie said with a little sigh. "If I could, I'd like to talk that way to papa."

"You shall learn then, darling," Violet said, caressing her with gentle fondness. "Would you like to begin now?"

"Oh, yes, mamma!" cried the child eagerly.

"Then bring me your slate, and I will set you a copy. Max and Lulu, would you like to bring your writing desks in here and let me give you any help you may need?"

Both assented to the proposal with thanks and were presently seated near her, each with open desk—a fresh sheet of paper spread out upon it and pen in hand.

"I think that until you become used to the business, it would be well to compose first with a pencil, then copy in ink," remarked Violet. "And here," taking it from a drawer in her writing desk as she spoke, "is some printing paper which takes a pencil mark much better than the more highly glazed paper which we use ordinarily in writing letters."

She gave each of them a pile of neatly cut sheets and a nicely sharpened pencil.

They thanked her and Max set to work at once.

Lulu sat playing with her pencil, her eyes on the carpet. "I don't know how to begin!" she exclaimed presently in an impatient tone. "What shall I say first, Mamma Vi?"

"Write down the date and then—then—suppose you dictate to me, if that will be any easier."

"Thank you, ma'am. I think it may be till I get into the way of it," Lulu said, handing over her paper and pencil with a sigh of relief.

"Now," said Violet encouragingly, "just imagine that you are sitting on your papa's knee and answering the question, 'What have you been doing all day?'"

"Well, papa, as soon as I was dressed and ready for breakfast, I went to Grandma Elsie's dressing room along with Rosie and the others to say Bible verses and hear Grandma Elsie talk about them and pray. Will that do, Mamma Vi?"

"Very nicely, dear. It is just what your papa wants, I think."

Lulu's brow cleared as she went on stating briefly the doings of the now closing day in the due order of their succession, Violet's pen nearly keeping pace with her tongue.

"And here we are—Max and Gracie and I—sitting with Mamma Vi in her boudoir, and she is writing for me the words I tell her. I'm to copy them off tomorrow," was the concluding sentence of this first entry in the little girl's diary.

"Will you hear mine, Mamma Vi, and tell me if it will do?" asked Max. Upon receiving permission, he read it aloud.

"It is very good indeed, Max," Violet said. "A good and true report, and well expressed. Now, if you and Lulu choose, you may bring your books here and study your lessons for tomorrow. If you need help from me, I shall give it with pleasure."

"But, Mamma Vi, it will be very dull for you to stay up here with us while the rest of the grown up people are having a nice time together in the parlor," said Max.

"You are very kindly thoughtful, Max," returned Violet, with a pleased look. "But I don't care to go downstairs for some time yet. Gracie begins to look weary; so I shall help her to bed and then answer your father's letter. Can't you imagine that I may prefer to talk to him for a little while rather than to anyone else, even if only with pen, ink, and paper?" she added with a charming blush and smile.

"Oh, yes, indeed! I know you're very fond of him. And I don't wonder, for I think he's the best and handsomest man in the world," cried Max enthusiastically, as both Lulu and Gracie chimed, "So do I."

"Then we are all in agreement so far," laughed Vi. "Come, Gracie, my little darling, I will be your maid tonight."

"No, no! Not my maid, but my dear, sweet, pretty mamma!" returned the little one, throwing her arms around Violet's neck and kissing her with ardent affection.

Lulu had risen to go for her books, but paused to say with a slight effort and heightened color, "Yes, Mamma Vi, you are sweet and pretty—and—very, very kind to us."

The child was by no means devoid of gratitude, though her pride and prejudice were hard to conquer. Expressions of gratitude and affection toward their young stepmother were far less frequent from her than from her siblings, but were perhaps all the more valued because of their rarity.

"Thank you, dear," returned Violet, happy tears glistening in her eyes. "If I am, it is because I love you both for your own and your father's sake."

She knew his heart always rejoiced in every demonstration of affection from his children toward her. So, in the letter she presently began writing, she recounted all that had been shown her that evening and others carefully treasured up in her memory for that purpose.

Chapter Ninth

*M*rs. Elsie Travilla and her family were greatly beloved in their own neighborhood. And as there had been no opportunity hitherto for showing attention to the three young, married ladies, there was quite an influx of callers for a week or two after the return to Ion. These calls were presently succeeded by a round of dinner and evening parties given in their honor.

The death of Mr. Love having occurred within the year, Zoe, of course, declined all such invitations. And it was only occasionally that Edward could be persuaded to go without her.

Violet accepted when it would have been deemed impolite or unkind to decline. Scarcely more than a bride, she felt a trifle forlorn going into society without her husband. She much preferred the quiet and seclusion of home.

This was to the advantage of the children, Max and Lulu, who thereby gained much fine assistance with their evening studies and Gracie a great deal of motherly care and cuddling.

So the duty of representing the family at these social gatherings devolved largely upon Lester and Elsie Leland, who laughingly declared themselves martyrs to the social reputation of the family.

"A very nice way to be martyred, I think," said Rosie. "I only wish they'd have the politeness to include me in their invitations."

"It would do you little good," remarked Mr. Dinsmore, "since you would not be allowed to accept, young lady."

"Are you quite sure, grandpa, that mamma wouldn't allow it?" she asked with an arch look up into his face.

"Quite. Since she never allows anything that I do not approve."

"Well," Rosie said, seating herself upon his knee and putting an arm around his neck, "I believe it isn't worthwhile to fret about it, since, as I'm not invited, I couldn't go anyhow."

"A sensible conclusion," he returned laughingly. "Fretting is an unprofitable business at any time."

"Ordinarily I should be very much of Rosie's opinion," Zoe said aside to her husband, "for I was always fond of parties. But, of course, just now I couldn't take the least pleasure in them," and she hastily brushed away a tear.

"No, love, I'm sure you could not," he said as he tenderly clasped the little hand she had laid in his. "But the truest, purest happiness is found at home. And," he added with a smile, "it is quite to the advantage of your plans for study that society can claim so little of your time and strength at present. You are doing so nicely that I am proud of my pupil."

She flushed with pleasure, but with a roguish smile, shaking her finger warningly at him, "Take care," she said, "and don't let the husband be lost in the tutor, or I shall—I shall—"

"What? Go over to grandpa as tutor?"

"Oh, no, no!" she cried, snatching her hand from his grasp and lifting both in mimic horror.

"What are you two chatting so cozily about in that far off corner?" asked Mrs. Leland's cheery voice from the midst of the larger group at the other side of the room.

"It's merely a little private confab between man and wife in which the public can have no interest," returned Edward.

"Quite a mistake, so far as this part of the public is concerned," said his mother, her soft hazel eyes gazing lovingly upon them. "But we won't pry into your secrets, only invite you to join our circle when you have finished your private chat."

For some weeks all went well at Ion. The family machinery worked smoothly, with no jarring or jostling—everybody in good humor and behaving kindly toward everybody else.

Max and Lulu made good progress in their studies and were able to give a good report of each day in their diaries, which, of their own accord, they brought each evening to Violet for her inspection.

She reminded them that they were not required to do so, but they answered that they preferred it. They wanted to know if she thought they were representing themselves as better than they really were.

She was glad to be able to answer with truth that she did not think so. She took pride that she could report them to their father as worthy of all praise in regard to both conduct and diligence in study.

"You have both been so pleasant tempered," she remarked in conclusion. "Lulu neither grumbling nor so much as looking sour over her tasks—even the sewing lessons, which I know are particularly distasteful to her. Dear child, you have been very good, and I know it will rejoice your father's heart to hear it," she added kissing the little girl's cheek.

Lulu's face flushed and her eyes shone. Mrs. Scrimp had always been ready to blame, never to praise, but with Mamma Vi it was just the other way. She was almost blind to faults, but particularly keen-sighted where virtues were concerned.

Violet turned to Max to find him regarding her with a wistful look.

"Well, what is it Max, my dear boy?" she asked laughingly as she gazed upon his little-boy face.

"Don't be partial, Mamma Vi," he answered. "I do believe a boy likes a kiss from a sweet, pretty lady that he has a right to care for, quite as well as any girl does."

"Then come and get it," she said, offering her lips. "Max, you may feel as free always to ask for it as if I were your own mother or sister."

Edward had, perhaps, the most trying pupil of all. She had done well at first, but as the novelty wore off, she lost her interest and found many excuses for not being prepared at the proper time for recitation. And if Edward so much as looked grave over the failure, Zoe was so hurt and felt herself so ill used that an extra amount of coaxing and caressing became necessary to restore her to her usual cheerfulness and good humor.

Edward was growing weary of the task, and at times he felt tempted to cease trying to improve the mind of his little wife. But, no, he could not do that if he would have her a fit companion for him intellectually as well as in other respects, for though she had naturally a fine mind, its cultivation had been sadly neglected.

He opened his heart to his mother on the subject, entreating her advice and assistance, but without finding fault with Zoe—Elsie would hardly have listened for a moment to that. She comforted him with words of encouragement to persevere in his own efforts and promises to aid him in every way in her power.

In pursuance of that object, she put in Zoe's way and recommended to her notice books that would be likely to interest and at the same time instruct her. She also considered her needs, as well as those of her pupils, in making her selections for the afternoon readings in the schoolroom.

There was much gained by the child-wife in these ways. The conversation of the highly educated and intelligent older members of the family of which she had now become a part helped her as well.

She was very desirous to become their equal in these respects, especially for Edward's sake. However, she was so much used to self-indulgence, so unaccustomed to self-control, that her good intentions and resolutions were made only to be broken till she herself was nearly ready to give up in despair.

Elsie was alone in her apartments one afternoon, an hour or more after dismissing her pupils to their play, when Zoe came to her with flushed cheeks, quivering lips, and eyes full of tears.

"What is wrong with you, my dear little daughter?" Elsie asked in tender, motherly tones, as she looked into the troubled face.

"Oh, mamma, I don't know what to do! I wish you could help me!" cried Zoe, dropping upon her knees at Elsie's feet and hiding her face on her lap. The tears fell fast now, mingled with sobs.

"Only tell me what is wrong, dear, and you shall have all the help I can give," Elsie said, smoothing the weeper's fair hair with a soft, caressing hand.

"Edward is vexed with me," sobbed Zoe. "I know he is, though he didn't say a word. But he looked so grave and walked away without even speaking."

"Perhaps he was not vexed with you, dear. Perhaps he was deep in thought about something that had no connection with his little wife, whom, as I very well know, he loves very deeply."

"No, mamma, it wasn't that. He had come in to hear me recite, and I was so interested in my fancy work that I'd forgotten to watch the time and hadn't looked at the lessons. So I told him and said I was sorry I wasn't ready for him. He didn't answer a word, but just looked at me as grave as a judge and turned round and walked out of the room."

"Surely, my dear Zoe, Edward does not insist upon his little wife learning lessons whether she is willing or not?" Elsie asked inquiringly and with a gentle caress.

"Oh, no, no, mamma! It has been my own choice, and I've no wish to give it up. But somehow there is always something interfering with my studying. Somebody calls, or I'm inclined for a ride, a drive, or a walk. Or I get engaged in sewing or fancy work, or my music, or a storybook that's too interesting to lay down till I reach the end. Mamma, I often wonder how it is that you find time for all these things and many others beside."

"Shall I tell you the secret of managing it, dear?" Elsie asked with an affectionate look and smile into the tear-stained face now uplifted to hers.

Zoe gave an eager assent, and Elsie went on. "It lies in doing things systematically—always putting duties first, giving to each its set time, and letting pleasures come in afterward. If I were you, my dear, I should have a regular study hour, putting it early in the day, before callers begin to come. I should not allow it to be lightly interfered with. No stitch should be taken in fancy work, no novel opened, no story paper glanced at, until each lesson for the day was fully prepared."

Zoe's face had brightened very much as she intently listened.

"Oh, mamma, I see now that that is just the way to do it!" she cried excitedly. "And I'll begin at once. I'll think over all the daily duties and make out a regular program, and I'll—"

"Strive earnestly to carry it out, you could say, yet not in your own strength alone," Elsie added as Zoe paused, leaving her sentence unfinished.

"Yes, mamma," she responded in a more serious tone. "And now, I'll run back to my room and try to be ready for Edward when he comes in again."

She set herself immediately to her tasks with unwonted determination to give her whole mind to them. Edward came in at length and was greeted with a bright look and the grand announcement in a tone of great satisfaction, "I'm quite ready for you now, Edward."

"I've been thinking we might perhaps as well give it up, Zoe," he answered gravely. "At least for the present, until you are done working upon those very fascinating Christmas things."

"Oh, no, don't!" she said flushing and looking ready to cry. "Try me a little longer, Ned. I've been talking with mamma, and I'm really going to turn over a new leaf and do just as she advises."

"Ah, if you have taken mamma into your counsels there is some hope," he said in a tone of hearty approval. "But we will have to put off the recitations until after tea. I must drive over to the Oaks to see Uncle Horace about a business matter, and I just came to ask you to go along."

"Oh, I'll be happy to!" she cried joyously, pushing the books aside and starting to her feet. "It won't take me a minute to don hat and cloak."

He caught her in his arms as she was rushing past him. Kissing her on the cheek and lips, he asked in tender tones, "My love, have I made you unhappy this afternoon?"

"Yes, for a little while, but I deserved it, Ned, and I don't mind it now if—if only you love your foolish, careless, little wife as well as ever in spite of all her faults."

"I love you dearly, dearly, my one own peculiar treasure," he responded with another caress of ardent affection as he let her go.

She was happy as a bird during their drive and full of enthusiasm in regard to her new plan, explaining it to Edward and asking his advice about the best division of her time. How much should be allotted to this duty and how much to that duty.

"I mean to rise earlier," she said. "And if I can't get time in that way for all I want to do, I'll shorten my rides and walks."

"No," he said, "I'm not going to have your health sacrificed even to mental improvement, and certainly not to fancy work. I shall insist on plenty of rest and sleep and an abundance of exercise in the open air for the dear, little woman I have taken to be my bride."

"Then, sir, you're not to be cross if the studies are not attended to."

"They will be if put before novels, fancy work, and other equally unnecessary employments."

"Well, I've said they shall be in the future. Oh, Ned," as she nestled closer by his side looking up lovingly into his face, "it's ever so nice to have somebody to take care of me and love me as you do! How could I ever do without papa, who always spoiled me so, if I hadn't you?"

"I hope you may never find out. I hope I may be spared to take care of you as long as you need me, little wife," he said pressing her closer to his side.

Rosie met them in the hall on their return to Ion.

"It's most tea time, Zoe," she said. "I think you'll not have any too much time for washing and changing your dress."

"Then I must needs make haste," returned Zoe, tripping up the stairs.

Edward, who was just then taking off his overcoat, turned a rather surprised, inquiring glance upon his little sister.

"Oh, yes," she said laughingly, "I had a reason for hurrying her away, because I want to tell you something. Cousin Ronald Lilburn is coming. He may even be here by tomorrow. Mamma heard he wasn't well, and she wrote and invited him to come and spend the winter with us. She's just had a letter saying he will come. Aren't you glad, Ned?"

"I'm very well pleased, Rosie, but why shouldn't Zoe have heard your announcement?"

"Because I wanted to warn you first not to tell her or the Raymonds about Cousin Ronald's special talent—shall we not keep it a secret at first, to have some fun?"

"Oh, yes!" he said with a good-humored laugh. "Well, I think you may trust me not to tell. But how about all the others? Walter, especially?"

"Oh, he doesn't remember anything about it. And grandpa and mamma and all the rest have promised not to tell."

"And you are quite sure my little Rosie may be trusted not to let the secret slip out unintentionally?" he asked, pinching her round, rosy cheek.

"I hope so," she said laughing and running away.

Opening the library door, Rosie spotted Lulu curled up in the corner of a sofa with a book. So she stepped in, shutting the door behind her.

Lulu looked up.

"Shall I disturb you if I talk?" asked Rosie.

"I'm ready to listen," answered Lulu, closing her book. "What have you to say?"

"Oh, only that we have a cousin—Ronald Lilburn—coming to visit, and I'm ever so glad. You would be, too, if you knew him."

"I've never heard of him," said Lulu. "Is he a boy? Is he older than Max?"

"I should think so!" cried Rosie with a merry laugh. "He has grown up sons, and he looks a good deal older than grandpa."

"Oh, pooh! Why should I care about his coming, then, Rosie?" exclaimed Lulu in a tone of mingled impatience and contempt.

"Why, because he is very nice and kind to us children and tells the loveliest stories about the brownies in Scotland and about Bruce and Wallace and the black Douglass and Robin Hood and his merry men, and—oh, I can't tell you what all!"

"Oh, that must be ever so nice!" cried Lulu, now as much pleased and interested in the news of the expected arrival as Rosie could desire.

Chapter Tenth

In which the children have some fun.

*I*n the uppermost story of the house at Ion was a large playroom furnished with a great variety of toys and games—indeed almost everything that could be thought of for the amusement of young folks from Walter up to Max.

But the greatest delight of the last named was in the deft handling of the tools in the adjoining apartment, called the boys' workroom. There he found an abundance of material to work upon, holly scroll and fret saws and a well-stocked tool chest.

Edward had given him lessons at the start and now he had become so expert as to be turning out some really beautiful pieces of carving, which he intended to give to his friends at Christmas.

Lulu, too, was learning scroll sawing, and she thought it far preferable to any sort of needlework—sometimes even more enjoyable than playing with her dolls.

They were there together one afternoon, both very busy and chatting and laughing as they worked away at their individual tasks.

"Max," said Lulu, "I'm determined to learn to do scroll sawing and carving just as well as you, so that I can make lovely things! Maybe I can contrive new patterns, or designs, or whatever they call 'em, and after a while make ever so much money—maybe enough to pay for my own clothes and everything—so that papa won't have to spend any of his money on me."

"Why, Lulu!" exclaimed her brother. "Do you think papa grudges the money he spends on you, or any of us?"

"No, I know he doesn't," she returned vehemently, "but can't you understand that I'd like him to have more to spend on himself?"

"Oh," said Max. "Well, that's right, I'm sure, and very thoughtful for a little girl like you. I do think you're splendid in some ways, Lu. And whether you make money by it or not, it will be a good thing to learn to do this work well. Papa says, 'knowledge is power,' and the more things we know how to do, the more independent and useful we will be."

Just then the door opened and Zoe, in riding hat and habit, poked her head around the door.

"Max, I'm going to take a ride into the village," she said. "And your Uncle Edward can't go with me as he intended. Will you?"

"Yes, Aunt Zoe, of course, if you want me," answered the boy promptly. He stopped his saw and sprang to his feet, for he was much gratified by the invitation. "I'll get ready as fast as I can. 'Twon't take over five minutes."

"Thank you. I'll wait for you in the parlor," said Zoe. "Lulu, would you like to go, too?"

"No, thank you, I had a ride this morning, and now I would like to finish this."

Max had left the room, and Zoe, drawing nearer to Lulu, exclaimed at the beauty of her work.

"Why, I never should have dreamed you could do it so well!" she said. "I don't believe I could."

Lulu's face flushed with pleasure, but she said modestly, "Perhaps you'd find, if you should try, that you could do it better. You do everything else better than I do."

"Quite a mistake," returned Zoe. "Though I ought to, as I'm so much older. But there, I dare say Max must be ready and waiting for me, so goodbye."

Zoe and Max met in the lower hall. "All ready, Max?" she asked.

"Yes—well, no, I must ask leave," and he ran into the parlor where all the ladies of the family were sitting busily working at their individual tasks.

It was of Grandma Elsie he asked permission and received it at once.

"Thank you, ma'am," he said. "Can I do anything for you in the town, ladies?"

"Yes," said Violet. "I have just broken a crochet needle. You may get me one to replace it."

She went on to give him directions about the size and where he would be likely to find it. Then, taking some money from her purse, "This is sure to be enough," she said, "but you may keep the change."

"Mamma Vi, I don't want pay for doing an errand for you," returned the boy, coloring. "It is a great pleasure, and it would be even if papa had not told me to wait on you and do all I could to fill his place."

"I don't mean it as pay, my dear boy," Violet answered with a pleased look, "but haven't I a right to make a little present now and then to the dear children who call me mamma?"

Max's face brightened.

"Yes, ma'am, I suppose so," he said. "Thank you. I'll take it willingly enough if it isn't pay, and I'm very proud to be trusted to buy something for you."

Edward was helping Zoe into the saddle as Max came hurrying out.

"Take good care of her, Max," he said, "I'm trusting you and Tom with my chiefest treasure."

"I'll do my best," Max said, mounting his pony that Tom was holding.

"Me, too, Marse Ed'ard; dere shan't nuffin hurt Miss Zoe," added the latter, giving Max the bridle, then mounting a third horse and falling behind the others as they cantered down the avenue.

A little beyond the gate the family carriage passed them with Mr. Dinsmore and a strange gentleman inside.

"Company," remarked Zoe. "I wonder who he is, and if he's come to stay any time. I think grandpa drove into the city to meet the afternoon train."

"Yes, I know he did," said Max.

Max had now learned to ride quite well and felt himself very nearly a man as he escorted Zoe to the village and, arriving there, went with her from store to store. Having executed Violet's commission, he then assisted Zoe back into the saddle, remounted, and returned with her to Ion.

It was very near the tea hour when they reached home. Zoe went directly to her own apartments to change her dress, but Max, without even waiting to take off his overcoat, hastened into the parlor to hand the crochet needle to Violet.

The ladies were all there, Rosie, Mr. Dinsmore, and an elderly gentleman, who Max recognized as the one he had seen in the carriage that afternoon.

The gentleman shook hands very kindly with the boy as Mr. Dinsmore introduced them, "Cousin Ronald, this is Max Raymond; Max, Mr. Lilburn."

"Ah ha, ah ha! Um, h'm! Ah ha! A fine looking lad," Mr. Lilburn said, still holding the boy's hand in a kindly grasp and gazing with evident interest into the bright young face. "I trust you and I are going to be good friends, Max. I'm not so young myself as I once was, but I like the company of the blithe young lads and lasses."

"Thank you kindly, sir," said Max, coloring with pleasure. "Rosie says you tell splendid stories about Wallace and the Bruce and Robin Hood and his merry men, too. I know I shall enjoy hearing them ever so much."

As he finished his sentence, he hastily thrust his right hand deep into the pocket on that side of his overcoat. For, much to his discomfiture and astonishment, a peculiar sound like the cry of a young puppy seemed to come from his pocket at that instant. Max colored violently.

"What is that? What have you got there, Max?" asked little Walter, pricking up his ears, while Violet asked with an amused look, "Have you been making an investment in livestock, Max?"

A query that seemed all the more natural and appropriate as the cluck of a hen came from the pocket on the other side of his overcoat.

Down went the left hand into that square. "No, Mamma Vi, there's nothing in my pockets," returned the boy with a look of great bewilderment.

"No, to be sure not," said Mr. Lilburn as the hen began to cluck behind Violet's chair, and the pup's cry was heard coming from underneath a heap of crocheting in Mrs. Dinsmore's lap—fairly startling her into uttering a little cry of surprise and dismay and springing to her feet.

Then everybody laughed, Rosie clapped her hands with delight, and Max glanced from one to another more mystified than ever.

"Never mind, Max," said Violet, "it's plain you are not the culprit who brought such unwelcome intruders here. Run up to your room now and make yourself ready for tea."

Max obeyed, but looking back from the doorway asked, "Shall I send one of the servants to turn out the hen and carry away the pup?"

"Never you mind, we'll attend to it, Max," said Mrs. Dinsmore.

"I'll find 'em. I can carry that pup out," said Walter, getting down from his grandpa's knee and beginning a vigorous search for it. The older people watched his frantic search with much amusement.

At length, having satisfied himself that neither it nor the hen was in the room, he concluded that they must be in Max's overcoat pockets and told him so the moment he returned.

"No, they are not, Walter, unless someone has put them there since I went upstairs," said Max. "But I don't believe they were actually here, Walter. I think they were only make believe."

"How make believe?" asked the tiny, little fellow in perplexity.

"Ask Mr. Lilburn."

"Come, explain yourself, young man," said that gentleman laughingly.

"I've certainly heard of ventriloquists, sir," said Max. "I don't know if you are one. But as the pup and the hen could only be heard and not seen, the only logical explanation would be that it must be the work of a ventriloquist."

"But you don't know for certain," said Rosie, coming to his side. "Max, please don't say anything to Zoe, or Lulu, or Gracie about it."

"I won't," he said as the door opened and the three entered, Zoe having overtaken the two little girls on their way downstairs after being dressed for the evening by the careful and expert Agnes.

"Mamma, do I look nice enough for your little girl?" asked Gracie, going to Violet's side.

"Very nice and sweet, my darling," was the quiet reply, accompanied by a tender caress.

Walter, hardly waiting until all of the necessary introductions were over, burst out eagerly, "Zoe, do you know where that pup is?"

"What pup?" she asked.

"I don't know his name."

"Well, what about him?"

"I thought he was in Max's pocket, but he wasn't and neither was the hen."

The tea bell rang at that instant, and Rosie, putting her lips to Walter's ear, whispered, "Do keep quiet about it and we'll have some fun."

"Will we, Rosie?" he replied with the look of mingled childlike wonder and pleasure. "Then, I'll keep quiet."

All through the meal Walter was on the lookout for the fun, but there was none beyond a few jests and pleasantries that were by no means unusual in their cheerful family circle.

"There wasn't a bit of fun, Rosie," he complained to her after all had returned to the parlor.

"Wait a little," she answered. "Perhaps it will come yet."

"Before I have to go to bed?"

"I hope so. Suppose you go and tell Cousin Ronald you want some fun. He knows how to make it. But be sure to whisper it in his ear."

Walter did as directed.

"Wait a wee bit, bairnie, and just see what will happen," Cousin Ronald answered in an undertone, and with a pleasant laugh, he lifted the little fellow to his knee.

Mr. Dinsmore sat near at hand, the ladies had gathered about the center table with their hand work. Lester Leland and Edward Travilla hovered near their wives—the one with a newspaper, the other merely watching the busy fingers of the fair workers as he made jesting comments upon what they were doing.

But presently there was a sudden commotion in their midst, one after another springing from her chair with a little startled cry. They were trying to dodge what, from the sound, seemed to be an enormous bumble bee circling round and round their heads and in and out among them. "Buzz! Buzz! Buzz!" Surely never a bumblebee buzzed so loudly before.

"Oh, catch it! Kill it, Edward!" cried Zoe, with a frantic rush to the farther side of the room. "Oh, here it comes after me! It's settling on my hair! Oh!"

"No, dear, it isn't, there is really nothing there, darling," Edward said soothingly, yet, with a laugh, for it suddenly occurred to him the real cause of the great disturbance.

"I believe it's gone," she said, drawing a long breath of relief as she turned her head this way and that. "But where did it go? And how strange for one to be flying about this time of year!"

The other ladies, exchanging amused glances, were drawing round the table again when a loud "cluck, cluck, cluck," came from a distant corner.

"Max, Max, catch her quick, 'fore she gets away!"

Max ran and hastily drew aside the curtain.

There was nothing there as Walter, Lulu, and Gracie, who had all rushed to the spot, perceived with amazement.

"Hark!" said Mr. Dinsmore, and as a deathlike silence fell upon the room the "cluck, cluck, cluck" was distinctly heard coming from the hall.

Out rushed the children and searched its whole length, but without finding the intruder.

Back they came to report their failure. Then dogs, big and little, barked and growled—now here, now there. Little pigs squealed, cats meowed, and mice squealed—from the corners, under the sofas and chairs, in the ladies' laps, in the gentlemen's pockets—yet not one could be seen.

For a while it made a great deal of sport, but at length little, feeble Gracie grew frightened and nervous. Running to "Mamma Vi," she hid her head in her lap with a burst of tears and sobs.

That put an end to the fun and frolic. Everybody sobered down instantly and kept very quiet while Grandpa Dinsmore carefully explained to the little weeper that Cousin Ronald had made all the sounds that had so excited and alarmed her. He promised her that there was really nothing in the room that could hurt or annoy her.

She lifted her head at last, wiped away her tears, and with a laugh that was really a sob, said, "I'll stop crying then, but I'm afraid everybody must think I'm a great baby."

"Oh no, dear!" said Grandma Elsie. "We all know that if our little girlie is easily troubled, it is because she is not well and strong like the rest of us."

"And I must beg your pardon for frightening you so, my wee bit of a bonny lassie," said Mr. Lilburn, stroking her hair. "I'll try to atone for it, one o' these days, by telling you and the other bairns the finest stories I know."

The promise called forth from the young folks a chorus of thanks and exclamations of delight. Walter excitedly added, "Won't you please tell one now, Cousin Ronald, to comfort Gracie?"

"A very disinterested request, no doubt, my little son," Elsie said laughingly, as she rose and took his hand to lead him from the room. "But it is high time both you and Gracie were in your nests. So bid good night and we will go. There'll be time enough for Cousin Ronald's stories."

Chapter Eleventh

At Christmas play, and make good cheer,
For Christmas comes but once a year.

—Tusser

*I*t was the day before Christmas. "When do our holidays begin, mamma?" asked Rosie, as she put her books neatly away in her desk after the last morning recitation.

"Now, my child. We will have no tasks this afternoon. Instead, I give my five little folks an invitation to drive into the city with me. How many will accept?"

"I, thank you, ma'am," "And I," "And I," came the chorus in joyous tones from one and another, for all were in the room. There was not one indifferent to the delight of a visit to the city, especially just at this time when the stores were so full of pretty things. Besides, who could fail to enjoy a drive with the kind, sweet lady some of them called mamma, others called Grandma Elsie?

"Then you may all be ready to start immediately after dinner," she said, glancing around upon them with a benign smile.

It was a still, bright day—actually quite mild for the season. There was no snow on the ground to make a sleigh ride possible, but the roads were good. They had fine horses and plenty of wraps. The ride in the softly cushioned, easy rolling carriage, whose large plate glass windows gave them a good view of the country first, then of the streets and shop windows of the city, was found very enjoyable.

They were not afraid to jest, laugh, and be merry as health, freedom from care, youthful spirits, and pleasing anticipations for the morrow inclined them to be.

Most of the Christmas shopping had been done days before, but some orders were left with grocers and confectioners, and Grandma Elsie treated generously to bonbons.

She allowed her children much greater latitude in such matters than her father had permitted her in her early years.

The Ion carriage had scarcely turned out of the avenue on its way to the city, when one of the parlors became the scene of great activity and mirth. A large Christmas tree was brought in and set up by the men servants; then, Lester, his Elsie, Violet, Edward, and Zoe proceeded to trim it.

That done, they gave their attention to the adornment of the walls with evergreens of that and several other rooms, completing their labors and closing the doors upon the tree some time before the return of the children.

"We shall have scarcely more than time to dress for tea," Grandma Elsie said, as the carriage drew up at the door. "So go directly to your rooms, my dears. Are you very tired, little Gracie?"

"No, ma'am, just a wee bit," said the child. "I'm getting so much stronger, and we've had such a nice time, Grandma Elsie."

"I'll carry you upstairs, little missy," said Tom, the servant man who opened the door for them, picking her up as he spoke.

"Bring her in here, Tom," Violet said, speaking from the door of her dressing room. "And will you come in, too, Lulu dear?"

Violet was very careful never to give Lulu an order. Her wishes when addressing her were always expressed in the form of a request.

Lulu complied at once, Tom stepping back for her to enter first.

She was in a high good humor, having enjoyed her drive extremely.

"Mamma Vi," she exclaimed. "We've had a splendid time! It's just delightful to be taken out by Grandma Elsie."

"Yes, I have always found it so," said Violet. "And how has your papa's baby girl enjoyed herself?" drawing Gracie toward her, as Tom set her down, and took off her hat.

"Oh, ever so much! Mamma, how beautiful you look! I wish papa was here to see you."

"That's just what I was thinking," said Lulu. "You are beautiful, Mamma Vi, and you always wear such pretty and becoming things."

"I am glad you approve my taste in dress," Violet said. "And what do you think of those?" with a slight motion of her hand in the direction of the bed.

Both little girls turned to look. Then with a little cry of surprise and delight, they hastened to give closer inspection to what they saw there—two pretty dresses of soft, fine, white cashmere, evidently intended for them, each with sash and ribbons laying upon it— Lulu's of rose pink, Gracie's a delicate shade of blue.

"Oh, Mamma Vi! Are they for us—for Gracie and me?" exclaimed Lulu.

"They were purchased and made expressly for my two dear little girls for them to wear tonight," said Violet. "Do they suit your tastes, dears?"

"They are just beautiful, my dear, sweet mamma," cried Gracie, running to her and smothering her with hugs and kisses.

"There, dear, that will do," said Violet, laughing, as she returned a hearty kiss. Then gently disengaging the child's arms from about her neck, she continued, "We must make haste to array you in them before the tea bell rings," and taking Gracie's hand, she led her toward the bed.

Lulu was standing there smoothing down the folds of her new dress, and noting with a thrill of pleasure how prettily the rich sash and ribbons contrasted with its creamy whiteness. "Mamma Vi," she said, looking up into her young stepmother's face, her expression a mixture of penitence and gratitude, "how good you and Grandma Elsie are to me! Indeed, everybody here is good to me, though I—I'm so bad tempered."

"You have been very good of late, dear," Violet said bending down to kiss her forehead, "and it is a dear delight to me to do all I can to make my husband's children happy."

Agnes now came to Violet's assistance and when the tea bell rang a few minutes later, the two little girls were quite ready to descend with their mamma to the supper room.

Grandma Elsie looked in on her way down, and Violet said sportively, "See, mamma, I have my dolls dressed."

"Yes," Elsie returned with a smile, "you were always fond of dressing dolls." And passing a hand over Gracie's curls and touching Lulu's cheek caressingly with the other, "These are better worth it than any you have had heretofore."

"Grandma Elsie," said Lulu in her fearless, straightforward way, while gazing with earnest, affectionate scrutiny into the fair face. "You don't look as if you could be mother to Mamma Vi and Aunt Elsie and Uncle Edward."

"Why, my child?" laughed the lady addressed. "Can't you see a resemblance?"

"Oh, yes, ma'am, but you look so young, not so much older than they do."

They were now passing through the upper hall. Walter had hold of his mother's hand and Rosie had just joined them.

"That is true," Rosie remarked. "And I am glad of it! I couldn't bear to have my dear, beautiful mamma grow old and wrinkled and grey."

"Yet it will have to be someday, Rosie, unless she is laid away out of sight before the time comes for those changes," the mother answered with a very gentle gravity.

There were various exclamations of surprise and pleasure from each of the children as they entered the supper room. Its walls were beautifully trimmed with evergreens, and bouquets of hothouse flowers adorned the table, filling the air with a delicious fragrance.

When the meal was over, all adjourned to the parlor usually occupied by the family when not entertaining company. This, too, they found trimmed with evergreens. While the children were looking about and commenting upon the tasteful display of the arrangements, the folding doors joining with another parlor were suddenly thrown open. This disclosed the grand achievement of the afternoon—the beautiful Christmas tree—tall, wide-spreading, glittering with lights and tinsel ornaments, gorgeous with bright colors, and every branch loaded down with gifts.

This glorious scene was greeted with a burst of admiration and applause from all present.

"What a beauty!" cried Rosie and Lulu, clapping their hands.

"And how large!" exclaimed Max. "Three times as big as any I ever saw before."

Walter and Gracie were no less enthusiastic in their admiration. "May we go close up, mamma?" asked the latter.

"Yes, 'course we may," said Walter seizing her hand. "We'll walk round it and look hard at the things, but not touch 'em."

The older people followed the lead of the little ones, and the tree was thoroughly examined by many pairs of eyes, gazed at from every point of view, and highly extolled before the work of despoiling it was begun.

The gifts were far too many to mention in detail. The older people seemed much pleased with some easels, brackets, and picture frames carved for them by Max and Lulu and with specimens of Zoe's and Rosie's handiwork in another line. Also, they were equally pleased with some little gems of art from the pencils and brushes of Lester, Elsie, and Violet, while the children were made happy with presents suited to the years and tastes of each.

Lulu was almost wild with delight over a set of pink coral, as nearly like that she had lost by her misconduct some months before, as Grandma Elsie had been able to find.

Then there was a beautiful thoroughly furnished workbox from Mamma Vi with a gold thimble in it, to encourage her in learning to sew. There was one for Gracie also exactly like it, except that Lulu's was lined with red satin and Gracie's with blue. Each had besides a new doll with a neat little trunk packed full of clothes made to fit and a box filled with pretty things to make up into doll clothes.

Max was greatly surprised and delighted to find himself the possessor of a watch, doubly valuable to him as his father's gift.

The gold thimbles for the little girls were also from their papa.

They had a number of other presents, but these were what they valued most highly.

It took quite a good while to distribute the gifts, and for each to examine and admire all his own and those of his neighbors. Then, Gracie, tired with excitement and the long drive of the afternoon, was ready to go to bed.

Mamma Vi went with her, as was her custom, and Max and Lulu followed. They had grown quite fond of Violet's somewhat sisterly, somewhat motherly talks with them at the close of the day. To her it was a source of deep joy and thankfulness that she could perceive she was influencing them—her dear husband's tenderly loved offspring—for the better.

She warmly sympathized in their pleasure tonight, chatted with them about what they had given and received, praised highly the picture frame and easel they had presented her, and instructed them in regard to the entries to be made in each of their diaries.

She left them in her boudoir busy with these when she returned to the parlor.

"Oh, Max," said Lulu, "how different Mamma Vi is from Aunt Beulah."

"Humph, I should think so," said Max. "Must have been made of a different kind o' dust. We certainly weren't so well off and happy last Christmas Eve, Lu."

"No, indeed! Gracie and I wanted a Christmas tree ever so much. We begged and coaxed for one, even if it was but a wee bit of a thing, but she wouldn't let us have it. She said it was just nonsense and a wicked waste."

"Just like her," remarked Max, in a tone of mingled aversion and contempt. "But let's not talk about her. I'd rather think of pleasanter subjects. Wasn't it splendid of papa to give me this watch?" pulling it out and gazing on it with pride and delight. "Isn't it a beauty?"

"Yes, and I'm glad as I can be that you have it, Max," Lulu responded affectionately. "And wasn't it good of him to give gold thimbles to Gracie and me? I shall try very hard to learn to sew nicely, to show him I'm grateful for it and all he does for me."

"That's right, Lu. Let's both do our best to improve all our opportunities so that we will make his heart glad. We can do that in another way, too."

"How?"

"By loving Mamma Vi and being as good to her as ever we know how."

"I do mean to, for she is good and kind to us," said Lulu in a frankly cordial tone.

"You were vexed at papa at first for marrying her," remarked Max with a roguish look. "But just suppose he'd taken Mrs. Scrimp instead."

"Oh, Max!" cried Lulu, her eyes flashing. "How can you even talk so? You know papa would never have thought of such a thing."

"I don't believe he would, but Ann told me once she knew Mrs. Scrimp would be glad enough to take him if he'd give her the chance. What would you have done if he had?"

"I don't know, Max, and it simply isn't even worthwhile considering," replied Lulu with the grownup air she occasionally assumed, much to Max's amusement. "But my writing's done and I'm going to bed for I'm tired and sleepy. So, my big brother, good night."

"Good night," returned Max. "I shan't be in a hurry to get to bed, for it won't be worthwhile to get up early to catch other folks, as all things have been given tonight. I almost wish they had let us wait till tomorrow morning."

Perhaps the remark was intended to throw Lulu off her guard, because at all events he was at her door with a "Merry Christmas," long before anyone else was stirring but the servants.

Lulu was awake, too, sitting up in bed and trying, in the dim light of the early Christmas dawn, to undo the wrapping on a small parcel she had found on her pillow.

Max had opened the door and given his greeting in subdued tones so that there might be no danger of disturbing any sleepers in the vicinity.

"Oh!" cried Lulu, in a voice of suppressed eagerness. "The same to you! Come in and see what Santa Claus has brought me!"

Max stepped in, closed the door, tiptoed to the window, raised the blinds, and drew back the white, lace curtains.

"Oh, Max, Max, just look and see!" cried Lulu, as he turned toward her again.

She had succeeded in her efforts and was now holding up her hand in an effort to display to advantage a very pretty gold ring.

"Yes, oh, I'm glad, Lu! And there's something else, isn't there?"

"Money! A good deal, isn't it, Max?" she asked, holding out a crisp new banknote.

"Five dollars," he answered, taking it to the light. "And I have the just same—found it on my pillow from papa—and I suppose yours is too. A gold pencil from Mamma Vi was there also."

"Yes, from papa," she said, examining the writing on the back of the envelope from which she had taken the note. "The ring's from Mamma Vi. She always finds out just what I want. I'd rather have had a ring than almost anything else."

"There, we have awakened her and Gracie, I'm afraid," said Max in a tone of self-reproach as the voices of the two were heard coming from the next room.

"Merry Christmas, Max and Lulu," both called out in cheery tones. The greetings were returned with added thanks to Violet for her gifts.

"I have some, too," Gracie said. "A lovely picture book and two kinds of money. I think I must be the richest little girl."

She had received a one-dollar bill, crisp and new like the others, and a quarter-eagle in gold. Try as they might, Max and Lulu could not convince her that the two did not amount to more than Max's or Lulu's five-dollar note.

The other members of the family had fared quite as well. The children had a very merry day, and the older people were quite happy.

There were fresh flowers on the graves in the family burial ground—even the dead had not been forgotten. Elsie Travilla had been early bending over the lowly mound that covered all that was mortal of her heart's best earthly treasure. Though the sweet face was calm and serene as was its wont, bearing no traces of tears, and the cheery words and bright smile came readily in sympathy with the mirth of the younger ones, her father and her older children noted the occasional far off look in the soft, hazel eyes. They knew that her thoughts were ever and anon with the husband of her youth.

Chapter Twelfth

*Oh, only those
Whose souls have felt this one idolatry,
Can tell how precious is the slightest thing
Affection gives and hallows! A dead flower
Will long be kept, remembrance of looks
That made each leaf a treasure.*

—Miss Landon

*T*he whole family connection living in the neighborhood had dined at Ion that Christmas day, and several had stayed to tea. But all had now gone, the good nights had been said among the members of the home circle, and Elsie Travilla was alone in her own apartments.

A little weary with the cares and excitement of the day, she was reclining on a sofa, in dressing gown and slippers, her beautiful hair unbound and rippling over her shoulders, beside her a jewelry box of ebony inlaid with mother-of-pearl.

The box stood open and the lamplight that fell upon its contents was flashed back from many a costly gem set in rings, brooches, lockets, and chains of gold.

She took them up one by one, gazing upon each for a minute or more with a smile, a sigh, or a falling tear, ere she laid it almost tenderly back in its proper place.

So absorbed was she in the contemplation of these mementos of the past and the memories called up by them, that she did not hear an approaching footstep. She had deemed herself quite alone, till a hand was laid gently on her head, and a voice said tenderly, "My darling!"

"Dear papa!" she responded, glancing up into his face with tear-dimmed eyes, as he stood at the back of her sofa, bending over her. "Let me give you a chair," and she would have risen to do so, but he forced her gently back.

"No, lie still, my darling. I will help myself." And coming round in front of her, he seated himself close by her side.

"Why look at these if it makes you sad, my child?" he asked, noticing her occupation.

"There is sometimes a sweetness in the tears called forth by pleasant memories of loved ones gone before, papa," she said. "These anniversaries will recall the dear husband who always remembered his little wife so kindly upon each, and there is a melancholy pleasure in looking over his Christmas gifts. I have them all, beginning with this—the very first. Do you remember it, papa? And the Christmas day when he gave it to me? The first Christmas that you were with me."

She was holding up a tiny, gold thimble.

"Yes, I think I do," he said. "I certainly remember the day—the first Christmas after my return from Europe, the first on which I heard myself addressed as papa by the sweetest of child voices, who called me that and wished me a Merry Christmas. Then the dearest, loveliest of little girls ran into my arms. Dear daughter, what a priceless treasure you have been to me ever since!" he added, bending over her and softly smoothing her hair. "It has always been a joy to call you mine."

She caught his hand and pressed it to her lips. "Yes, dear, dear father! And to me to be so called. We loved one another very dearly then, each was all the other had, and I think our mutual love has never been less because of the other many tender ties God has given us since."

"I am sure you are right, daughter, but at that time," he added with a smile, "you were not willing to share your father's love with another—at least not with another that you suspected was trying to win it. Do you remember how you slipped away to your bed without bidding your papa good night and cried yourself to sleep?"

"Yes, foolish child that I was!" she said with a low musical laugh. "And how you surprised me the next morning by your knowledge of my fears and then set them all at rest, like the dear, kind father that you were and always have been."

"No, not always," he sighed.

"Yes, papa, always," she said with a playful tenderness. "I will insist upon that, because even when most severe with me, you did what at the time you deemed your duty and believed it to be for my good."

"Yes, that is true, my dear, forgiving child! And yet, I can never think of the suffering you endured during the summer that succeeded that Christmas without keen remorse."

"Yet, long before the next Christmas came I was happier than ever," she said, looking up into his face with a smile full of filial love. "It was the first in our own dear home at the Oaks. You remember, don't you, papa? You gave me a lovely set of pearls—necklace and bracelets—and this," taking up a pearl ring, "was Edward's gift. Mr. Travilla he was to me then, and no thought of one day becoming his wife had even so much as entered my head. But years afterward he told me that he had had it in his mind even then, had already resolved to wait till I grew up and win me for his wife if he could."

"Yes, he told me after you were grown and he offered himself, that it had been love at first sight with him—little child that you were when he first made your acquaintance. That surprised me, though somewhat less than the discovery that you fancied one so many years your senior."

"But so good, so noble, so lovable!" she said. "Surely it was not half so strange, papa, as that he should fancy a foolish young thing such as I was then—not meaning that I am yet very greatly improved," she added with a tearful smile.

"I am fully satisfied with you just as you are," he said, bending down over her and touching his lips two or three times to her forehead. "My darling, my first-born and beloved child! No words can express the love and tenderness I feel for you, or my pity for the grief that is beyond my power to relieve."

"Dear papa, your sympathy is very sweet," she said in tremulous tones. "It is very, very sweet in itself, and it helps me to a fuller realization of the depth of meaning in those sweet words, 'Like as a father pitieth his children, so the Lord pitieth them that fear Him.'"

"You cannot be wholly miserable while the Father's precious love and pity are yours, my dear child, even if all earthly loves should be taken from you—God forbid that should ever happen."

"No, papa, dearly as I loved my husband, I am happy in that divine love still mine, though parted from him. And dearly as I love you and my children, I know that were you all taken from me, I could still rejoice in the love of Him who died for me, and who has said, 'I am with you always, even unto the end of the world.' 'I will never leave thee nor forsake thee.' 'I have loved thee with an everlasting love.'"

Silence fell between them for some time, both seemingly wrapped in thought. Then, Mr. Dinsmore inquired, "You will go to Roselands tomorrow?"

"Yes, papa, if you go, as I heard you say you intended, and nothing happens to prevent it. Rosie was particularly delighted with Cal's invitation," she added, smiling up at him. "I had been telling her the story of those Christmas holidays that we have been discussing, and she and the other children naturally now want to look upon the scenes of all those important events."

"It will not be by any means her first visit to Roselands," he remarked in a tone of surprise.

"Oh, no, sir! Only the first after hearing of those interesting episodes in her mother's life."

"But the house is not the same."

"No, sir, yet the hall and parlors, your rooms and mine are about where and what they were in the old house."

"Ah! Well, I hope Rosie will enjoy it. And that you may do so, too. I shall leave you now, begging you to go at once to bed. Good night, daughter."

"Good night, my dearest, best of fathers," she responded, putting her arms around his neck as he stooped to give her a parting caress.

Calhoun and Arthur Conly were now the joint proprietors of Roselands. Aunt Maria, an old Negress born and bred on the estate, was their housekeeper, and she managed it so well that they found themselves as comfortable as in the days of their mother's administration.

They, with one younger sister and brother, were all of the once large family now left to occupy the old home—these younger two were there now only for the Christmas holidays. At their close, they would again return to distant boarding schools. Ella, the sister, was eighteen; Ralph, two years younger.

The house from whence the mother and the grandfather had been carried out to their last long home but a few months before, could not be made the scene of mirth and jollity, but to a day of quiet social exchange with near and dear relatives and friends none could object. So, the family at Ion had been invited to dine there the next day, and they had readily accepted the invitation.

Lulu had been greatly interested in Grandma Elsie's story and secretly wished such a party of children as had been told of had been invited to Ion for these holidays. But she did not covet such a father as Mr. Dinsmore. He was much too strict and severe, she thought, even with all his cuddling, and she would far rather have her own papa. Still Grandma Elsie's lot, when a little girl, seemed to her an enviable one. She was beautiful and so rich and had a nice, old mammy always ready to wait on and do everything for her. And Lulu was sure she wouldn't have minded much when such a father as Mr. Dinsmore was vexed with her—no indeed! She almost thought she should enjoy trying her strength in a tilt with him even now.

Lulu was a rebel by nature and always found it difficult to combat the inclination to defy authority and assert her entire independence of control.

But fortunately, this inclination was in great measure counterbalanced by the warmth of her affections. She was ready to love all who treated her with justice and kindness, and her love for her father was intense. To please him, she would do or endure almost anything. That more than any other influence had kept her on her good behavior all these weeks.

She had sometimes rebelled inwardly, but there had been no greater outward show of it than a frown or a pout that had soon vanished under the kind and gentle treatment she received at the hands of Grandma Elsie and Mamma Vi.

Captain Raymond would have been very much gratified could he have seen how, not only she, but all his children, were improving morally, mentally, and physically in the wholesome atmosphere of their new home.

Gracie had gained largely in both strength and vivacity; her cheeks were rounder and rosier than when she came to Ion; her eyes were brighter, too. And though not yet the equal of her brother and sister to extreme exercise, she could enjoy quiet play and would often laugh quite merrily.

She had grown very fond of Dr. Conly, or Cousin Arthur, as he told her to call him, as had he of his little patient. She frequently hovered about him during Christmas day and received from him a special invitation to Roselands.

"You and your mamma are to be my particular guests," he said. "And if, my dear, you fail to enjoy yourselves it shall be from no fault of mine."

"We shall not fail," Violet said with confidence. "How could we with Cal and yourself for our hosts, Arthur?"

The day proved propitious. All members of the Ion house went and all enjoyed their visit. Though, to the older ones there was at first a feeling of subdued sadness in thinking of the old grandfather, whose chair was now vacant, and who had been wont to greet their coming with words of cordial welcome.

It was after dinner that Rosie laid claim to her mother's promise.

"Well," said Elsie glancing dreamily about, "this parlor where we are all sitting occupies the same part of the house and is almost exactly like the one where the scenes I told you of took place."

"What scenes?" asked Dr. Conly, drawing near with a look of interest.

Mr. Dinsmore, too, turned to listen.

"I have been telling all of the children about the Christmas holidays at Roselands the first winter after my father returned from Europe," she answered. "It was before you were born, Cousin Arthur, while your mother was still a very young girl."

"Mamma," asked Rosie, "where was grandpa sitting when you went to him and confessed that Carry Howard cut off one of your curls?"

"Near yonder window. Do you remember it, papa?" she asked looking smilingly at him.

"Yes, I think I have forgotten very little that ever passed between us. You were a remarkably honest, conscientious child—would come and confess wrong doing that I should never have known or suspected, even when you thought it likely I should punish you severely for it."

"Now, mamma," said Rosie, "won't you go into the hall and show us just where papa caught you, kissed you, and gave you the gold thimble? And then your room and grandpa's?"

"Arthur, have we your permission to roam over the house?" Elsie asked, turning to him.

"Yes, provided you will let me go along, for I am as much interested as the children."

"Come, then," she said, rising and taking Walter's hand. Rosie, Lulu, and Gracie kept close to her, and Mr. Dinsmore and Arthur followed along behind.

Pausing in the hall, she pointed out the precise spot where the little scene had been enacted between herself and him who would someday be her husband, telling her story between a smile and a tear. She then moved further up the stairs with her little procession.

Opening a door, she said, "This was my room, or rather my room was here before the old house was burned down. It looks just the same, except that the furniture is different."

Then passing on to another, "This was papa's dressing room. I passed many happy hours here, sitting by his side or on his knee. It was here that I opened the trunk full of finery and toys he brought me a few days before that Christmas. Papa," turning to smile at him, as she pointed to a closed door on the farther side of the room, "do you remember my imprisonment in that closet?"

"Yes," he answered with a remorseful look. "But do not speak of it. How very ready I was to punish you for the most trifling fault."

"Indeed, papa," she answered earnestly. "It was no such trifle, for I had disobeyed a plain order not to ask a second time for permission to do what you had once forbidden."

"True, but I now see that a child so sensitive, so conscientious, and so affectionate as you were, would have been sufficiently punished by a mild rebuke."

"A year or two later you discovered and acted upon that," she said with an affectionate look up into his face. "But at this time you were a very young father. When I remember how you took me on your knee by the fire there and warmed my hands and feet as you cuddled and caressed me and what a nice evening I had with you afterward, I could almost wish to go through it again."

"Hark! What was that?" exclaimed Rosie.

Everyone else paused to listen.

There was a sound of sobbing as of a child in sore distress, and it seemed to come from the closet.

"There's somebody shut up in there now," Walter said in a loud, excited whisper. "Grandpa, can't she be let out now?"

Arthur strode hastily across the room and threw the closet door open wide.

There was no one there. They glanced at each other in surprise and perplexity.

"Ah, ha! Um, h'm! Ah, ha! The lassie's no there, eh?" said a voice behind them. Turning quickly at the sound, who should they see but Mr. Lilburn standing in the open doorway leading into the hall.

"But we know all about her now, sir, don't we?" asked Arthur with a laugh in which he was joined by everyone present.

Chapter Thirteenth

Evil communications corrupt good manners.

—1 CORINTHIANS 15:33

The one major drawback upon Max's perfect enjoyment of his new home was the lack of a companion of his own age and sex. The only boys in the family connection or even among the near neighbors were nearly grown to manhood or very little fellows.

Therefore, when Ralph Conly came home for the Christmas holidays, and though four years older than himself, at once admitted him to a footing of intimacy, Max was both pleased and flattered.

Ralph's manner was a bit more condescending than was altogether agreeable, but that seemed not inexcusable, considering his superiority in years and knowledge of the world.

At Ion, Max played the part of the host, taking Ralph up to his own bedroom to show him his books and other treasures, to the boys' workroom, out to the stables to see the horses, and about the fine grounds.

Today at Roselands, it was Ralph's turn to entertain. He soon drew Max away from the company in the parlors, showed him the horses and dogs, then invited him to take a walk.

It was near dinner time when they returned. After dinner he took Max to his room and producing a pack of cards, invited him to play.

"Cards!" exclaimed Max. "I don't know anything about playing with them and don't want to."

"Why not? Are you too pious?" Ralph asked with a sneer, tumbling them out in a heap upon the table.

"I've always been taught that men gamble with cards, and that gambling is very wicked and quite disgraceful, as bad as getting drunk."

"Pooh! You're a muff!"

"I'd rather be a muff than a gambler any day," returned Max with spirit.

"Pshaw! 'Tisn't gambling unless you play for money, and I haven't asked you to do that and don't propose to. Come now, take a hand," urged Ralph persuasively. "There isn't a bit more harm in it than in a game of ball."

"But I don't know how," objected Max.

"I'll teach you," said Ralph. "You'll soon learn and will find it good sport."

At length Max yielded, though not without some qualms of conscience that he tried to quiet by saying to himself, "Papa never said I shouldn't play in this way. He said only that gambling was very wicked, and I must never go where it was done."

"Have a cigar?" asked Ralph, producing two, handing one to Max and proceeding to light the other. "You smoke, of course. Every gentleman I know of does."

"Thank you, I don't care if I do," he said and was soon puffing away as if accustomed to it.

But it was not very many minutes before he began to feel sick and faint, then in turns, trembling and growing giddy.

He tried to conceal these sensations and fought against them as long as possible. But at length, finding he could endure it no longer, he threw the stump of the cigar into the fire and said as he rose, "I—I feel sick. I must get out into the air."

He took a step forward, staggered, and would have fallen, if Ralph had not jumped up and caught him in time.

"Here, I'll help you to the bed and open the window," he said. "Never smoked before, eh? Well, don't be discouraged. I was deathly sick the first time myself."

"I'm half blind and awfully sick," groaned Max, as he stretched himself on the bed. "Does it last long? Can a fellow get over this sickness without taking any medicine?"

"Oh, yes, you'll be all right after a little while."

But Max was not all right when a servant came to the door to say that he was wanted downstairs as the party from Ion were about to return home.

"Think you can get down with the help of my arm?" asked Ralph.

"Don't b'lieve he kin, Marse Ralph," remarked the servant, gazing earnestly at Max. "What's de mattah wid de young gentleman? He's white as de wall, and his eyes looks like glass."

"Hush, Sam! You'll frighten him," whispered Ralph. "Run down and ask my brother Arthur to come up. Don't let anybody else hear you."

Max tried to rise, but only fell back again sicker than ever.

"Oh, but I'm sick, and how my heart beats!" he said. "I can't possibly sit up, much less walk downstairs. What will Mamma Vi and the rest say? I'm afraid Grandpa Dinsmore will be very angry with me."

"He hasn't any right to be," said Ralph. "'Tisn't wicked to smoke. But I'll tell Art not to let him know what made you sick."

Just then the doctor came in. Sam had met him in the hall.

"What's the matter?" he asked. "Sick, Max? Ah, you've been smoking?" sniffing the air of the room and glancing at the boy's pallid face.

"Tell him it isn't dangerous, Art," laughed Ralph. "Oh, I do believe he's dreadfully scared."

"No, I'm not!" protested Max indignantly. "But I'm sick, and giddy, and half blind. I had never smoked before and didn't know how it would sicken me so."

"How many cigars did you smoke?" asked Arthur, taking hold of his wrist.

"Only half of one," said Ralph. "He threw the rest of it in the fire."

"The best place for it," said Arthur. "Don't be alarmed, my boy, the sickness and all the other bad effects will pass off after a while—all the sooner if you are breathing pure air. Ralph, open the door into the hall and the one opposite. Then ring for Sam to kindle a fire in that room." As he spoke he took Max in his arms and, Ralph proceeding them to open the doors, carried him into an unoccupied bedroom, laid him on a couch, and covered him up carefully to guard against his taking cold.

"No need to ring for Sam. The fire's laid all ready to kindle," remarked Ralph as he glanced at the open grate.

He struck a match, and in another minute the flames were leaping up right merrily.

Meantime a report that Max was sick had reached the parlor, and Mr. Dinsmore, his daughter, and granddaughter came up to express their sympathy and see for themselves how serious the illness was. Their faces were full of anxiety and concern till they learned the cause of the sickness, when they evidently felt much relieved.

"Dear boy, I'm sorry you are suffering," Violet said leaning over him. "But I hope you will never try it again."

"Papa smokes," he said. "So I thought it was all right for me."

"No," said Mr. Dinsmore. "A grown person may sometimes do safely what is dangerous for a younger one. You have my sympathy this time, Max, but if ever you make yourself sick in the same way again, I don't think I shall pity you at all. He will hardly be able to go home today, Arthur?"

"No, sir, leave him here in my care. Tomorrow he will probably be quite recovered and I will drive him over in my gig."

"Would you like me to stay with you, Max?" Violet asked, laying her cool hand on his forehead.

"Or me?" asked her mother.

"No, thank you, Grandma Elsie and Mamma Vi," he said. "You are both very kind, but Walter and Gracie wouldn't know what to do without you, and I shall do very well."

"Yes," said Ralph. "I'll help Art take care of him. I ought to, as I gave him the cigar that sickened him."

Mr. Dinsmore and the ladies than bade goodbye and went downstairs, the doctor accompanying them and leaving the two boys alone together.

"Have you begun to get over it, old fellow?" asked Ralph.

"No, I'm wretchedly sick," said Max. "I think I've had enough tobacco to last me all my days."

"Oh, pshaw! It won't be half so bad next time and pretty soon won't sicken you at all."

"But what is there to gain or pay me for all the suffering it does cause?"

"Well, it seems sort o' babyish not to smoke."

"Does it? I've never seen Grandpa Dinsmore smoke, and I don't believe he ever does, nor Uncle Edward, nor Uncle Horace, neither."

"No, they don't and Art doesn't, but they're all sort o' pious old fogies," Ralph said with a coarse sort of laugh.

"I wouldn't talk so about my own relations if I were you," returned Max in a tone of disgust.

"Of course, I shouldn't let anybody else say a word against them," said Ralph.

Arthur's entrance put an end to the conversation. He inquired of Max if the sickness were abating. Then, sitting down beside him, he said, "Boys, I want to talk to you a little about this silly business of smoking and chewing."

"I've never chewed," said Max.

"I'm glad to hear it, and I hope you never will, or smoke again either. How would you like, Max, to have a cancer on your lip?"

"Cancer, sir? I wouldn't choose to have one for anything in the world."

"Then don't smoke, especially a short pipe, for it often causes cancer of the lip. I cut one out of a man's lip the other day. Not long ago, I saw a man die from one after months of agonizing pain. Tobacco contains a virulent poison, and though some people use it for many years without apparent injury, it costs many others loss of health, and even of life. It weakens the nerves and the action of the heart and is a fruitful source of dyspepsia."

"Pooh! I don't believe it will ever hurt me," boldly declared Ralph.

"I think it will," said Arthur. "You have not attained your growth and therefore are the more certain to be injured by its use."

"Max, my boy, I admire your father greatly—particularly his magnificent physique."

Max flushed with pleasure.

"Do you not wish to be like him in that? As tall and finely developed?"

"Yes, sir. Yes, indeed! I want to be like papa in everything and in every way!"

"Then eschew tobacco, for it will certainly stunt your growth!"

"But papa smokes," repeated Max.

"Now, but probably he did not until grown," said Arthur. "And very likely he sometimes now wishes he had not contracted the habit. Now I must leave you for a time, as I have some other patients to visit."

"I told you he was an old fogy," said Ralph as the door closed on his brother. He added with an oath, "I believe he wouldn't allow a fellow a single bit of pleasure if he could help it."

Max started and looked at Ralph with troubled eyes. "I didn't think you would swear," he said. "If you do, I—I can't be friends with you, because my father won't allow it."

"I don't often," said Ralph, looking ashamed. "I won't again in your company."

Chapter Fourteenth

Be sure your sin will find you out.

—Numbers 32:33

Gracie and Walter were in the playroom. They had been building block houses for an hour or more, when Gracie said, "I'm tired, Walter. I'm going in yonder to see the things Max and Lulu are making." So, she rose and sauntered into the wood-working room.

She watched the busy carvers for some minutes, but growing bored, went in search of Violet in their own apartments.

She found no one there but Agnes busily putting away some clean clothes, fresh from the iron.

"Where's mamma?" asked the little girl.

"In de drawin' room, Miss Gracie. Comp'ny dar."

"Oh, dear!" sighed Gracie. "I just wanted her to talk to me."

"'Spect you hab to wait till de comp'ny gone," returned Agnes, picking up her empty clothesbasket and leaving the room.

Gracie wandered disconsolately about the rooms, wishing the callers would go and mamma come up. Presently she paused before the bureau in Violet's dressing room and began fingering the pretty things on it.

She was not usually a meddlesome child but just now was tempted to mischief from the lack of something else to interest and employ her.

She handled the articles carefully, however, and did them no damage till she came to a beautiful cut-glass bottle filled with a costly perfume of which she was extravagantly fond.

Violet had frequently given her a few drops on her handkerchief without being asked and never refused a request for it.

Gracie, seized with a desire for it, took a clean handkerchief from a drawer and helped herself, saying aloud by way of quieting her conscience, "Mamma would give it to me if she was here. She always does, and I'll be careful not to break the bottle."

She was pouring from it as she spoke. Just at that instant she heard a step in the hall without and a sound as if a hand was laid on the doorknob.

The sound so startled her that the bottle slipped from her fingers and, striking the bureau as it fell, lay in fragments at her feet. Its contents were spilled upon the carpet and the air of the room was redolent of the delicious perfume.

Gracie, naturally a timid child who shrank from everything like reproof or punishment, stood aghast at the mischief she had wrought.

"What will mamma say?" was her first thought. "Oh, I'm afraid she will be so vexed with me that she'll never love me any more!" And the tears came thick and fast, for mamma's love was very sweet to the little, feeble child who had been so long without a mother's care and tenderness.

Then arose the wish to hide her fault. Oh, if she could only replace the bottle, but that was quite impossible. Perhaps, though, there might be a way found to conceal the fact that she was the author of the mishap. She did not want to have anyone else blamed for her fault, but she would like not to be suspected of it herself.

A bright thought struck her. She had seen the cat jump on that bureau a few days before and walk back and forth over it. If the pussy were left in the room alone there that afternoon, she might have done the same thing again and knocked the bottle off upon the floor.

It would be no great harm the little girl reasoned, trying to stifle the warnings and reproaches of her conscience, if she should let the cat take the blame.

Mamma was kind and wouldn't have the pussy cat beaten, and pussy's feelings wouldn't be hurt at all, either, by the suspicion.

She hurried out in search of the cat. Finding her in the hall, she pounced on her, carried her into the dressing room, and left her there with all the doors shut. That way she could not escape till someone going in would find the bottle broken and think the cat had done it.

This accomplished, Gracie went back to her play in the playroom and tried to forget her wrongdoing in the interesting employment of dressing her dolls.

Lulu presently left her carving and joined her. Max had gone out for a ride upon his little pony.

While chasing the cat, Gracie had not perceived a little, woolly head thrust out of a door at the farther end of the hall—its keen, black eyes closely watching her movements.

"Hee, hee, hee!" giggled the owner of the head as Gracie secured pussy and hurried into the dressing room with her. "Wondah what she done dat fer!"

"What you talkin' 'bout, you sassy chile?" asked Agnes, coming up behind the little girl on her way to Mrs. Raymond's apartments with another basket of clean clothes, just as Gracie reappeared and hurried up the stairs to the story above.

"Why, Miss Gracie done come pounce on ole Tab while she paradin' down de hall an' ketch her up an' tote her off into Miss Wilet's dressin' room an's lef' her dar wid de do' shut on her. What for you s'pose she done do dat?"

"Oh, go 'long! I don' b'lieve Miss Gracie didn't do no sich ting!" returned Agnes.

"She did den, I seed her," asserted the little maid positively. "Mebbe she heerd de mices runnin' 'round an want ole Tab for to ketch 'em."

"You go 'long and tend to yo' wuk, Bet, you lazy chile," responded Agnes, pushing past her. "Miss Wilet an Miss Gracie dey'll min' dere own consarns widout none o' yo' help."

The child made no reply, but stole on tiptoe after Agnes down the hall.

Violet was coming up the front stairway and reached the door of her dressing room just in advance of the girl. Opening it, she exclaimed at the powerful perfume that greeted her nostrils. Then, catching sight of the bottle laying in fragments on the floor, "Who could have done this?" she asked in a tone of surprise not wholly free from displeasure.

"De cat mos' likely, Miss Wilet," said Agnes, setting down her basket and glancing at the puss who was stretched comfortably on the rug before the fire. "I s'pect she's been runnin' ober de bureau, like I see her do mor'n once 'fo' dis."

"She looks very quiet now," remarked Violet. "And if she did the mischief it was certainly not intentional. Please don't leave her shut up in here again, Agnes."

"She didn't do it, Agnes didn't," volunteered Betty, who had stolen in after them. "It was Miss Gracie, Miss Wilet, I seed her ketch ole Tab out in de hall dere and put her in hyar, an' shut de do onto her, an' go off upstairs."

A suspicion of the truth flashed into Violet's mind, but she put it resolutely from her. She would not believe Gracie capable of slyness and deceit.

Violet wanted the little girl and sent Betty up with a message to that effect, bidding her make haste. And when she had attended to that errand, Violet bid her brush up the broken glass and put it in the fire.

Betty ran nimbly up to the playroom and, putting her head in at the door, said with a grin, "Miss Gracie, yo' mamma wants you come down to her dressin' room."

"What for?" asked Gracie with a frightened look.

"Dunno, I s'pect you fin' out when you gits dar sho 'nuff."

"Betty, you're a saucy thing," said Lulu.

"S'pect mebbe I is, Miss Lu," returned the little maid with a broader grin than before, apparently considering the remark quite complimentary. She held the door open for Gracie to pass.

"Miss Gracie," she asked as she followed Gracie down the stairs, "what fo' you shut ole Tab up in de dressin' room? She's done gone an' broke Miss Wilet's bottle what hab de stuff dat smell so nice, an' cose Miss Wilet she don' like dat ar."

"What makes you say I put her in there, Betty?" said Gracie.

"Kase I seed you, hee, hee, hee!"

"Did you?" asked Gracie, looking still more alarmed than at the summons to the dressing room. "Don't tell mamma, Betty. I'll give you a penny and help you make a frock for your doll if you won't."

Betty's only answer was a broad grin and a chuckle as she sprang past Gracie to open the door to the dressing room.

Violet, seated on the farther side of the room, looked up with her usual sweet smile. "See, Gracie dear, I am making a lace collar for you and I want to try it on you to see if it fits."

"Now, Betty, get a dust pan and brush and sweep up the glass. Don't leave the least bit of it on the carpet, lest some one should tramp on it and cut their foot."

"Someone has broken that cut-glass perfume bottle you have always admired so much, Gracie, dear. Aren't you sorry?"

"Yes, I am, mamma. I never touch your things when you are not here."

The words were out almost before Grace knew she meant to speak them, and she was terribly frightened and ashamed. She had never thought she would be guilty of telling a lie. She hung her head, her cheeks aflame.

Violet noted the child's confusion with a sorely troubled heart.

"No, dear," she said very gently. "Gracie, I did not suspect you, but if ever you should meet with an accident, or yield to temptation to do some mischief, I hope you will come and tell me about it at once. You need not fear that I will be severe with you, for I love you very dearly, little Gracie."

"Perhaps it was the cat who knocked it off the bureau, mamma," said the child, speaking low and hesitantly. "I've seen her jump up there several times before."

"Yes, so have I, and she must not be left alone in here any more."

Betty had finished her work and was sent away. Agnes, too, had left the room, so that Violet and Gracie were quite alone.

"Come, dear, I am quite ready to try this on," Violet said, holding up the collar. "There, it fits very nicely," she said as she put it on the child and gently smoothed it down over her shoulders. "But what is the matter, my darling?" for tears were trembling on the long, silken lashes that swept Gracie's flushed cheeks.

At the question they began to fall in streams, while the little chest heaved with sobs. She pulled out a handkerchief from her pocket to wipe her eyes, and a strong whiff of perfume greeted Violet's nostrils, telling a tale that sent a pang to her heart.

Gracie was instantly conscious of it, as she, too, smelled the telltale perfume and stole a glance at her young stepmother's face.

"Oh, mamma!" she sobbed, covering her face with her hands. "I did pour a little on my handkerchief 'cause I knew you always let me have it, but I didn't mean to break the bottle. It just slipped out of my hands, fell, and broke."

Violet held her to her heart and wept quite bitterly over her.

"Mamma, don't cry," sobbed the child. "I'll save up all my money till I can buy you another bottle, just like that."

"Oh, Gracie, Gracie, it's not that!" Violet said when emotion would let her speak. "I valued the bottle as the gift of my dear, dead father, but I would rather have lost it a hundred times over than have my darling tell a lie. It is so wicked! God hates lying. He says, 'All liars shall have their part in the lake that burneth with fire and brimstone.' 'He that speaketh lies shall not escape.' He says that Satan is the father of lies, and that those who are guilty of lying are the children of that wicked one.

"Have you forgotten how God punished Gehazi for lying by making him a leper and struck Ananias and Sapphira dead for the same sin? Oh, my darling, my darling, it breaks my heart to think you have both acted and spoken a falsehood!" she cried, clasping the child still closer to her and weeping over her afresh.

Gracie, too, cried bitterly. "Mamma, mamma," she said, "will God never forgive me? Will He send me to that dreadful place?"

"He will forgive you if you are truly sorry for your sin because it is dishonoring and displeasing to Him, and if you ask Him to pardon you for Jesus' sake. And He will take away the evil nature that leads you to commit sin, giving you a new and good heart, and take you to heaven when you die.

"But no one can go to heaven who is not first made holy. The Bible bids us follow 'holiness without which no man shall see the Lord.' And Jesus is a Savior from sin. 'Thou shalt call His name Jesus, for He shall save His people from their sins.' Shall we kneel down now and ask Him to save you from yours?"

"Yes, mamma," sobbed the child.

Violet's prayer was short and to the point. Then she held Gracie for some time in her arms, while they mingled their tears together.

At length, she said, "Gracie, dear, I believe God has heard our prayer and forgiven you. I am sure He has if you are truly sorry in your heart and asked with it, and not only with your lips, for forgiveness. But I want you to stay here alone for an hour and think it all over quietly—I mean about your wrongdoing and God's willingness to forgive for Jesus' sake. Think about the fact that we could not have been forgiven and saved from sin and hell if the dear Savior had not died for us the cruel death of the cross.

"Oh, think what a dreadful thing sin must be that it could not be blotted out except by Jesus suffering and dying in our stead! And think how great was His love for us, when He was willing to lay down His own life that we might live!"

Then with a kiss of tender motherly love, she went out and left the child alone.

Gracie was sincerely penitent. She had always been taught that lying was a dreadful sin and had never before told a direct falsehood. But, while in her former home, Mrs. Scrimp's faulty management joined to her own natural timidity had tempted her to occasional slyness and deceit. From these the descent to positive untruth was easy.

Violet's faithful dealing with Gracie, and even more the evidence of her deep distress because of the sin against God of which her darling had been guilty, had so convicted the child of the heinousness of her conduct that she was sorely distressed because of it. And on being left alone, knelt down again and pleaded for pardon with many bitter tears and sobs.

She had risen from her knees and was lying on a couch, still weeping, when Lulu came into the dressing room.

"Why, Gracie, whatever is the matter?" she asked, running to the couch and bending over her little sister in tender concern.

"Don't ask me, Lulu. I don't want to tell you," sobbed Gracie, turning away her blushing and tear-stained face.

"Mamma Vi has been scolding or punishing you for some little naughtiness, I suppose," said Lulu frowning slightly.

"No, she hasn't!" cried Gracie indignantly. Then, hastily correcting herself, "except that she said she wanted me to stay here alone for a while. So you must go and leave me."

"I won't till you tell me what it was all about. What did you do, Gracie? Or was it something you didn't do?"

"I don't want to tell you, 'cause you wouldn't ever do such a wicked thing, and you—you'd despise me if you knew I'd done it," sobbed Gracie.

"No, I wouldn't. You are better than I am. Papa said I was worse than you and Max both put together. So you needn't mind my knowing."

"I meddled and broke mamma's pretty bottle that her dead father gave her, but she didn't scold me for that. Not a bit—but—but 'cause I tried to put the blame on the cat, and—and said I—I never touched her things when she wasn't here," she sobbed.

"Oh, Gracie, that was wicked! To say what wasn't true! I think papa would have whipped you. For I've heard him say if there was anything he would punish severely in one of his children, it was telling a lie. But don't cry so. I'm sure you're sorry and won't ever do it again."

"No, no! Never, never! Mamma hugged me up in her arms and cried hard 'cause I'd been so wicked. And she asked Jesus to forgive me and make me good, so I shouldn't have to go to that dreadful place. Now go away, Lulu, 'cause she said I must stay alone."

"Yes, I will, but stop crying or you'll be sick," Lulu said, kissing Gracie. She then left the room and went to her own to make herself neat before going down to join the family at tea.

Her thoughts were busy with Gracie and her trouble while she brushed her hair, washed her hands, and changed her dress. "Poor little weak thing, she was frightened into it, of course, for it's the very first time she ever told an untruth. I suppose Mamma Vi must have looked very cross about the broken bottle, and she needn't, I'm sure, for she has plenty of money to buy more. Such a shame! But I just knew she wouldn't always be kind to us."

Thus, Lulu worked herself up into a passion, quite forgetting, in her unreasonable anger, how very mild was the punishment Violet had decreed to Gracie—if indeed it was meant as such at all. It was so much less severe than the one she herself had said their father would have been likely to administer had he punished Gracie.

Max was riding without companion or attendant. He had taken the direction of the village, but not with any thought of going there. Until, as he reached its outskirts, it occurred to him that he was nearly out of wood for carving, and that this would be a good opportunity for laying in a supply.

The only difficulty was that he had not asked leave before starting, and it was well understood that he was not at liberty to go anywhere—visiting or shopping—without permission.

"How very provoking!" he exclaimed aloud. "I haven't time to go back and ask leave. A long storm may set in before tomorrow, and so my work be stopped for two or three days. I'll just go on, for what's the difference anyhow? I'm almost there, and I know I'd have gotten leave if I'd only thought of asking before I left."

So he went, made his purchase, and set off home with it.

He was rather late. A storm seemed brewing, and as he rode up the avenue Violet was at the window looking out a little anxiously for him.

Mr. Dinsmore, hearing her relieved exclamation, "Ah, there he is!" came to her side as Max was in the act of dismounting.

"The boy has evidently been into town making a purchase," he said. "Had he permission from you or anyone, Violet?"

"Not from me, grandpa," she answered with a little reluctance.

"Did you give him leave, Elsie?" he asked, turning to face his daughter. "Or you, wife?"

Both answered in the negative, and so, with a stern countenance, Mr. Dinsmore went out to the hall to meet the delinquent.

"Where have you been, Max?" he asked in no honeyed accents.

"For a ride, sir," returned the lad respectfully.

"Apparently, not merely for a ride," Mr. Dinsmore said, pointing to the package in the boy's hand. "You did not pick that up by the roadside. Where have you been?"

"I stopped at Turner's just long enough to buy this wood that I shall need for carving tomorrow. I should have asked leave, but forgot to do so."

"Then you should have come home and left the errand for another day. You were well aware that in going without permission you were breaking rules. You will go immediately to your room and stay there until this time tomorrow."

"I think you're very hard on a fellow," muttered Max, flushing with mortification and anger as he turned to obey.

Lulu, coming down the stairs, had heard and seen it all. She stood still for a moment at the foot of the stairway, giving Mr. Dinsmore a look that, had it been a dagger, would have stabbed him to the heart, but as his back was turned, he did not see. Then, just as the tea bell rang, she turned and began the ascent again.

"Why are you going back, Lulu? Did you not hear the supper bell?" asked Mr. Dinsmore.

"Yes, sir," she answered, facing him again with flashing eyes. "But if my brother is not to go to the table neither will I."

"Oh, very well," he said. "You certainly do not deserve a seat there after such a speech as that, young lady. Go to your own room and stay there until you find yourself in a more amiable and respectful mood."

It was exactly what she had intended to do, but because he had so ordered it, it instantly became the thing she did not want to do.

However, she did as had been bidden and went into her room. Closing the door after her, not too gently, she said aloud with a stamp of her foot, "Hateful old tyrant!" then walked on into Violet's dressing room where her sister still was.

Gracie had lain down upon a sofa and wept herself to sleep, but the supper bell had awakened her. And she was crying again. Catching sight of Lulu's flushed, angry face, she asked what was the matter.

"I wish we could go away from these people and never, never come back again!" cried Lulu in her vehement way.

"I don't," said Gracie. "I love mamma and Grandma Elsie and Grandma Rose and Grandpa Dinsmore, too, and—"

"I hate him! I'd like to beat him! The old tyrant!" interrupted Lulu, in a burst of passion.

"Oh, Lu, I'm sure he's been kind to us. They're all kind to us when we're good," expostulated Grace. "But what has happened to make you so angry, and why aren't you eating your supper with the rest?"

"Do you think I'd go and sit at the table with them when they won't have you and Max there, too, Gracie?"

"What about Max? Oh my, did he do something wrong, too?"

"No, it wasn't anything wicked. He just bought some wood for his carving projects with some of his own money."

"But maybe he went without leave?" Gracie replied inquiringly.

"Yes, that was it. He forgot to ask. A very little thing to punish him for, I'm sure. But Mr. Dinsmore—I sha'n't call him grandpa—says he must stay in his room till this time tomorrow."

"Why," said Gracie, "that's worse than mamma's punishment for me for—for doing such a wicked, wicked thing!"

"Yes, she's not such a cruel tyrant. He'd have beaten you black and blue. I hope she won't tell him about it."

A terrified look came into Gracie's eyes, and she burst out crying again.

"Oh, Gracie, don't!" Lulu entreated, kneeling down beside the sofa and clasping her arms about her. "I didn't mean to frighten you so. Of course, Mamma Vi won't. If she meant to she'd have done it long before now, and you'd have heard from him, too, I'm certain."

A step came along the hall, the door opened, and Agnes appeared bearing a large, silver tray.

"Ise brung yo' suppah, chillens," she said, setting it down on a table.

Then lifting a stand and placing it near Gracie's couch, she presently had it covered with a snowy cloth and a dainty little meal arranged upon it—broiled chicken, stewed oysters, delicate rolls, hot buttered muffins and waffles, canned peaches with sugar and rich cream, fresh sponge cake, and an abundance of rich, sweet milk.

The little girls viewed these dainties with great satisfaction and suddenly discovered that they were very hungry.

Agnes set up a chair for each, saw them begin their meal, then left the room, saying she would be back directly with more hot cakes.

"There, Gracie, you needn't be the least bit afraid you're to be punished any more," remarked Lulu. "They'd never have sent us such a supper as this if they wanted to punish us."

"Do you want to run away from them now?" asked Gracie. "Do you think Grandpa Dinsmore is so very, very cross with us?"

"He's too hard on Max," returned Lulu. "Though not so hard as he used to be on Grandma Elsie when she was his own little girl. And perhaps papa would be just as hard as he is with Max."

"But 'tisn't 'cause they like to make us sorry, except for when we're naughty, so that we'll grow up good, you know," said Gracie. "I'm sure our dear papa loves us, every one, and he wouldn't ever make us sorry except just to make us good. And you know we can't be happy here, or go to heaven when we die, if we're not good."

"Yes, I know," said Lulu. "I'm not a bit happy when I'm angry and stubborn, but for all that I can't help it."

Chapter Fifteenth

Happy in this, she is not yet so old
But she may learn.

—Shakespeare

*V*iolet, meeting her grandfather on the way to the supper room, gave him an anxious, troubled, inquiring look, which he answered by a brief statement, given in an undertone, of what had passed between himself and Max and Lulu.

"All of them!" sighed the young stepmother to herself, "all three of them at once! Ah, me!"

Though Mr. Dinsmore had spoken lowly, both his daughter and Zoe had heard nearly all he said, and as they sat down to the table the one looked grieved and distressed, the other angry.

During the meal Zoe never once addressed Mr. Dinsmore, and when he spoke to her, she answered as briefly as possible and not in a very pleasant or respectful tone.

Edward noticed it and looked at her in displeased surprise. Then, becoming aware of the absence of the Raymonds, asked, "Where are Max, Lulu, and little Gracie?"

He had not heard the story of their disgrace, having come to the supper room a little later than the others and directly from his own room.

For a moment the question, addressed to no one in particular, remained unanswered. Then Mr. Dinsmore said, "Max and Lulu are in disgrace. I know nothing about Gracie, but presume she is not feeling well enough to come down."

Zoe darted an angry glance at him.

Violet looked slightly relieved. She had not spoken at all of Gracie's wrongdoing and did not want anyone to know of it.

"I may send the children their supper, grandpa?" she said inquiringly, with a pleading look.

"Do just as you please about it," he answered. "Of course, I would not have growing children go fasting for any length of time—certainly not all night—for that would be to the injury of their health. And I leave it to you to decide how luxurious their meal shall be."

"Thank you, grandpa," she said and at once gave the requisite order.

Meanwhile Max had obeyed the order to go to his room in almost as angry and rebellious a mood as Lulu's own. He shut the door, threw down his package, tore off his overcoat and stamped about the floor for a minute or two, fuming and raging.

"I say it's just shameful! Abominable treatment! I'm tired of being treated like a baby, and I won't stand it! The idea of being shut up here for twenty-four hours for such a trifle! Oh, dear!" he added, dropping into a chair. "I'm as hungry as a bear. I wonder if he doesn't mean to let me have any supper? I don't believe Mamma Vi would approve of his starving me altogether—no, nor Grandma Elsie, neither. I hope they'll manage to give me something to eat before bedtime. If they don't, I believe I'll try to bribe Tom when he comes to see to the fire."

It was not long before he heard Tom's step on the stairs, then his knock on the door.

"Come in," he answered, in cheerful tones. Then, as he caught sight of the tray full of good things, such as his sisters were supping upon, he cried, "Hurrah! Tom, you're a brick! But who sent it?"

"Miss Wilet, and she says if dars not nuff ob it to satisfy yo' appetite, you's to ring for mo'."

"All right. Tell Mamma Vi I'm much obliged," said Max.

"Very good prison fare," he added to himself as he fell to work, Tom having withdrawn. "I've good reason to be fond of Mamma Vi, and she's fond of her grandfather. I s'pose I'll have to forgive him for her sake," he concluded, quite restored to his usual good humor and laughing gleefully at his own jest.

"Oh, Lulu," exclaimed Gracie, struck with a sudden recollection, as she laid down the spoon with which she was eating her oysters. "You know I was to stay alone. You oughtn't to have come in here."

"Pooh! Your time was up a good while ago," returned Lulu. "And Mamma Vi must have expected me to come in here to eat supper along with you. I hope she has sent as good a one to poor Maxie."

Violet went directly from the supper room to her own apartments where she found the girls quietly talking together, while Agnes gathered up the remainders of their repast and carried it and the dishes away.

"I hope you enjoyed your supper, my dears," she said softly.

They both said they had and thanked her for it.

"And I didn't deserve it, mamma," added Gracie, her tears beginning to fall again. "Oh, I'm sorry, so very sorry! Please, mamma, forgive me."

"I have entirely forgiven the sin against me, my darling," whispered Violet, folding her close to her heart. "And I trust God has forgiven your far greater sin against Him. Now do not cry any more, or you will make yourself sick, and that would make me very sad."

Lulu was sitting nearby fighting a battle with pride and passion, in which ere long she came off the conqueror.

"Mamma Vi," she said with determination, "I didn't deserve it either, and I'm sorry, too, for being angry at your grandfather and saucy to him."

"Dear child," said Violet, drawing her to her side and kissing her with affectionate warmth, "how glad I am to hear you say that. May I repeat your words to grandpa as a message from you?"

Again Lulu struggled with herself. Perhaps it was only the thought that this was the easiest way to make an apology, which she knew would probably be required of her sooner or later, that helped her to conquer yet again.

Her entry in her diary in regard to the occurrence was, "I was a little saucy to Grandpa Dinsmore because he was hard on Max for just a little bit of a trifle, but I've said I'm sorry, and it's all right now."

Edward and his grandfather, having a business matter to talk over together, repaired to the library on leaving the table. However, Zoe, instead of going as usual to the parlor with the others, went to her own rooms.

She had seen Violet, who was a little in advance of her, going into hers, and only waiting to take a little package from a closet, she ran lightly up to Max's door. She tapped gently on it and then in her eagerness, opened it slightly with a whispered, "It's only Zoe, Max. May I come in?"

"Yes, indeed," he answered, springing forward to admit her and hand her a chair. "How good of you to come, Aunt Zoe."

"No, I did it to please myself. You know you've always been a favorite with me, Max, and I want to know what this is all about."

Max told her.

"It's a perfect shame!" she exclaimed indignantly. "I can't see the least bit of harm in your going to the store and buying what you did. You weren't wasting the pocket money that you had a right to spend as you pleased. Grandpa Dinsmore is a—a—rather tyrannical, I think."

"It does seem hard to have so little liberty," Max said, discontentedly. "But I don't know that he's any more strict, after all, than papa."

"Well, I must run away now," said Zoe, jumping up. "Here's something to sweeten your imprisonment," she said, putting a box of confectionery into his hand. "Goodbye," and she tripped away.

She met her husband in the hall upon which their rooms opened. "Where have you been?" he asked coldly and with a suspicious look.

"That's my affair," she returned, flushing and with a saucy, little toss of her pretty head.

He gave her a glance of mingled surprise and displeasure. "What has come over you, Zoe? Can you not give me a civil answer to a simple question?"

"Of course I can, Mr. Travilla, but I think it's a pretty story if I'm to be called to account as to where I go even about the house."

"Nothing but a guilty conscience could have made you look at my question in that light," he said, leaning against the mantel and looking down severely at her as she stood before him, for they were now in her boudoir. "I presume you have been to Max's room, condoling with and encouraging him in his defiance of grandpa's authority. Now, let me tell you, I won't allow it!"

"It makes no difference whether you allow it or not," she said, turning away with a contemptuous sniff. "I'm my own mistress."

"Do you mean to defy my authority, Zoe?" he asked with suppressed anger.

"Yes, I do. I'll do anything in the world for love and coaxing, but I won't be driven. I'm your wife, sir, not your slave."

"I have no desire to enslave you, Zoe," he said, his tone softening. "But you are so young, so very young for a married woman, that you surely ought to be willing to submit to a little loving guidance and control."

"I didn't perceive much love in the attempt you made just now," she said, seating herself and opening a book.

He watched her for a moment. She seemed absorbed in reading, and he could not see that the downcast eyes were too full of tears to distinguish one letter from another.

He left the room without another word, and hardly had the door closed on him when she flung the book from her, ran into the dressing room, threw herself on a couch, and cried as if her heart would break.

"He's all I have, all I have!" she moaned. "And he's beginning to be cruel to me! Oh, what shall I do! What shall I do! Papa, papa, why did you die and leave your darling all alone in this cold world?"

She hoped Edward would come back again presently, say he was sorry for his brutal behavior, and try to make peace with her by coaxing and cuddling. But he did not. So after a while she gave up expecting him, undressed, went to bed, and cried herself to sleep, feeling that she was a sadly ill-used wife.

Meanwhile Edward had returned to the library for a time, then gone into the family parlor, hoping and expecting to find Zoe there with the rest. But the first glance around the room showed him that she was not there.

He made no remark about it, but sitting down beside his mother, he tried to interest himself in the evening paper handed him by his grandfather.

"What have you done with your wife, young man?" asked his sister Elsie sportively. "We have seen nothing of her since supper."

"I left her in her room," he answered in a tone that there seemed a shade of annoyance.

"Have you locked her up there for very bad behavior?" asked Rosie laughing.

"Why, whatever do you mean, Rosie?" he returned, giving the child an angry glance, and colored deeply.

"Oh, I was only funning, of course, Ned. So you needn't look so vexed about it. That's the very way to excite suspicion that you have done something to her," and Rosie laughed gleefully.

But to the surprise of mother and sisters, Edward's brow darkened and he made no reply.

"Rosie," said Violet lightly, "you are an incorrigible tease. Let the poor boy alone, can't you?"

"Thank you, Mrs. Raymond," he said with a forced laugh. "But I wouldn't have Rosie deprived of her sport."

"I hope," remarked Mrs. Travilla, with a kindly, though grave look at her youngest daughter, "that my Rosie does not find it sport to inflict annoyance upon others."

"No, mamma, not by any means, but how could I suppose my wise oldest brother would care for such a trifle?" returned the little girl in a still sprightly tone.

"My dear," said her mother, "it is the little things—little pleasures, little vexations—that far more than the great make up the sum total of our happiness or misery in life."

Edward was silent during the rest of the evening, and his mother, watching him furtively and putting that and that together, felt sure that something had gone wrong between him and his young wife.

When the good nights had all been said and the family scattered to their rooms, he lingered behind, and his mother, who had left the room, perceived it, returning to find him standing on the hearth and gazing moodily into the fire.

She went to him and laid her hand gently on his shoulder, saying in her sweet, low tones, "My dear boy, I cannot help seeing that something has gone wrong with you. I don't ask what it is, but you have your mother's sympathy in every trouble."

"It is unfortunately something you would not want me to repeat even to you, my best and dearest of mothers. But your assurance of sympathy is sweet and comforting nevertheless," he said, taking her in his arms with a look and manner so like his father's, that tears sprang unbidden to her eyes.

"Ah," he said presently with a sigh that betrayed more than he was aware of, "my father was a happy man in having such a woman for his wife!"

"A good husband makes a good wife, my boy," she returned, gazing searchingly yet tenderly into his eyes. "And I think no woman with any heart at all could have failed to be such to him."

"I am not worthy to be his son," he murmured, the hot blood mounting to his very hair.

There was a moment or more of silence. Then she said, softly caressing his hair and cheek as she spoke, "Edward, my son, be very patient, very gentle, forbearing, and loving toward that orphan child—the care of whom you assumed of your own free will. She is the little wife you have promised to love and cherish to life's end."

"Yes, mother, I have tried very earnestly to be all that to her, but she is such a child that she needs guidance and control. I simply cannot let her show disrespect to you or my grandfather."

"She has always been both dutiful and affectionate to me, Ned, and I have never known her to say a disrespectful word to or about your grandfather."

"Did you not notice the looks she gave him at the table, tonight? The tone in which she replied when he spoke to her?"

"I tried not to do so," she said with a smile. "I learned when my first children were young that it was the part of wisdom to be sometimes blind to venial faults. Not," she added more gravely, "that I would ever put disrespect to my father in that category, mind you. But we must not make too much of a little girlish petulance, especially when excited by a generous sympathy with the troubles of another."

The cloud lifted from his brow. "How kind of you to say it, mother dear! Kind to her and to me. Yes, she is very fond of Max, quite as if he were a younger brother. I suppose it is very natural that she should sympathize with him when in disgrace."

"And having been coddled and indulged by her father; allowed to have her own way in almost everything; and seldom, if ever, called to account for her doings, comings, and goings, she can hardly fail to think my father's rule strict and severe."

"True," Edward responded with a small sigh. "Grandpa is a strict disciplinarian, yet so kind and affectionate with it all that one cannot help loving him in spite of the strictness."

"So I think. And now, good night, my dear son, I must go. And perhaps your little wife is looking and longing for your coming. She is very fond and proud of her young husband," and with a motherly kiss and smile, she left him.

Edward paced the floor for several minutes with thoughtful air then went upstairs to Zoe's boudoir.

She was not there or in the dressing room. He took up a lamp and went into the adjoining bedroom. Shading the light with his hand, he drew near the bed with noiseless step.

She lay there sleeping, tears on her eyelashes and her pillow wet with them. His heart smote him at the sight. She looked such a mere child and so sweet and innocent that he could hardly refrain from imprinting a kiss upon the round, rosy cheek and the full, red lips.

And he longed for reconciliation, but it seemed cruel to wake her. So, I shall attend to it first thing in the morning he said to himself. He set the lamp down in a distant part of the room and prepared for rest.

Max had spent the evening over his books and diary. His entry in the latter was a brief statement of his delinquency, its punishment, and his resolve to be more obedient in the future.

He had just wiped his pen and put it away, when Grandma Elsie came for a little motherly talk with him, as she often did at bedtime.

He received her with a mortified, embarrassed air, but her kind, gentle manner quickly restored his self-possession.

"I was sorry indeed," she said, "to hear that our boy Max had become a breaker of rules and so caused us the loss of his company at the table and in the parlor."

"I had thought the loss was all on my side, Grandma Elsie," he returned with a bright, pleased look. "I didn't suppose anybody would miss me unpleasantly."

"Ah, you were quite mistaken in that. We are all fond of you, Max."

"Not Grandpa Dinsmore, I'm sure," he said, dropping his eyes and frowning.

"Why, Max, tell me what else could induce him to give you a home here and be at the trouble of teaching you every day?"

"I thought it was you who gave me a home, Grandma Elsie," Max said in a softened tone and with an affectionate look at her.

"This is my house," she said. "But my father is the head of the family. Without his approval I should never have asked you and your sisters here—much as I desire your happiness, and fond of you as I certainly am."

"You are very, very good to us!" he exclaimed with warmth. "You do so much for us! I wish I could do something for you!"

"Do you, my dear boy?" she said smiling and softly patting his hand, which she had taken in hers. "Then, be respectful and obedient to my father. And to your mamma—my dear daughter. Nothing else could give me so much pleasure."

"I love Mamma Vi!" exclaimed Max. "I'm sure there couldn't be a sweeter lady. And I like Grandpa Dinsmore, too, but—don't you think now he's very strict and ready to punish a fellow for a mere trifle, Grandma Elsie?"

"I dare say it seems but a trifle to you for a boy of your age to go into town and do an errand for himself without asking leave," she replied. "But that might lead to much worse things. The boy might take to loitering about the town and fall into bad company and so be led into I know not what wickedness. For that reason parents and guardians should know all about a boy's comings and goings."

"That's so, Grandma Elsie," Max said reflectively. "I don't mean to get into bad company ever, but papa says I'm a heedless fellow, so perhaps I might have done it before I thought. I'll try to keep to rules after this."

"I hope so, for both your own sake and ours," she said. Then, with a sweet mother's kiss, she bade him a good night.

Chapter Sixteenth

O jealousy! Thou merciless destroyer,
More cruel than the grave! What ravages
Does thy wild war make in the noblest bosoms!

—MULLET

Edward stretched himself beside Zoe, but not to sleep for hours, for ever and anon she drew a sobbing breath that went to his very heart.

"Poor little thing!" he sighed. "I must have acted like a brute to grieve her so deeply. I should not have undertaken the care of a child who I knew had been spoiled by unlimited coddling and indulgence, if I could not be more forbearing and tender with her. If, instead of a show of authority, I had tried reasoning and coaxing, doubtless the result would have been different, and she would have been saved all this. I am ashamed of myself! Grandpa might possibly have acted so toward a wife, but my father never, I am sure."

He was really fond of his little wife, loving her with a protective love as something peculiarly his own. She was to be guided and molded to suit his ideas and wishes, so that she might eventually become the perfectly congenial companion. A companion who was capable of understanding and sympathizing in all his views and feelings. She was, however, not that companion yet.

He began to fear that she might never attain to that, that perhaps his sudden marriage was a mistake that would ruin the happiness of both for life.

Tormented thus, he turned restlessly on his pillow with many a groan and sigh, nor closed an eye in sleep till long past midnight.

He was sleeping very soundly when, at about sunrise, Zoe opened her eyes.

She lay still for a moment listening to his quiet breathing, while memory recalled what had passed between them previous to her retiring.

"And there he lies and sleeps just as soundly as if he hadn't been playing the tyrant to the woman he promised to love and cherish to life's end," she said to herself with a flash of anger and scorn in her eyes. "Well, I don't mean to be here when he wakes. I'll keep out of his way till he's had breakfast, for they say men are always complete savages on an empty stomach."

She slipped cautiously out of the bed, stole quietly into the next room, washed and dressed herself in riding habit and hat, went downstairs, ordered her pony saddled and brought to the door, and was presently galloping away down the avenue.

Edward had requested her never to go alone, to always to take a servant as an attendant—even if she had one of the children with her, and especially if not. But she disregarded his wishes in this instance, partly from a spirit of defiance, partly because she much preferred a solitary ride and could not see that there was any danger in it.

It was a bright spring morning, the air just cold enough to be delightfully bracing. Men were at work in the fields, orchards were full of bloom and fragrance, forest trees leafing out, and springing grass and flowers making the roadsides lovely.

Zoe's spirits rose with every mile she traveled—the perfume of the flowers, the songs of the birds, and all the sweet sights and sounds of nature that greeted eye, ear, and every sense, filled her with joy. How could she, so young and full of life and health, be unhappy in so beautiful a world?

So keen was her enjoyment that she rode farther than she had intended. Time passed so quickly that, on looking at her watch, she was surprised to find that she would hardly be able, even at a gallop, to reach Ion by the breakfast hour.

She was a little disturbed at that, for everybody was expected to be punctual at meals. Grandpa Dinsmore was particular about it, and she did not wish to give Edward fresh cause for displeasure.

As she galloped swiftly up the avenue she was surprised to see him pacing the veranda to and fro, watch in hand, while his horse stood near, ready saddled and bridled.

As she drew rein close by the veranda steps, Edward hastily returned his watch to its fob, sprang forward, and lifted her from the saddle.

"Good morning, little wife," he said with an affectionate kiss as he set her down, still keeping his arm about her. "I was not so kind as I might, or should have been last night, but you will not lay it up against your husband, love?"

"No, of course not, Ned," she returned, looking up into his face flushed and happy that so loving an apology had been given her in place of the reproof she expected. "And you won't hate me because I was cross when you were?"

"Hate you, love! No, never! I shall love you as long as we both live. But I must say goodbye. I am summoned away on important business and shall have hardly time to catch the next train."

"You might have told me last night," she pouted. And with another kiss, he took his arm from her waist and turned to leave her.

"I did not receive the summons till half an hour ago," he answered, hastily mounting his steed.

"When will you come back?" she asked.

"I hope to be with you by tea time this evening. Au revoir, darling."

He threw her a kiss and was gone, galloping so rapidly away that in a minute or two he was out of sight—all the more speedily to her because her eyes were blinded with tears as she stood motionless, gazing after him.

"Never mind, dear child, it is for only a few hours, if all goes well," said the kind, sweet voice at her side.

"Yes, mamma, but—oh, I wish he never had to go away without me! And why couldn't I have gone with him this time?" she sobbed, beginning to feel herself quite aggrieved, even though the idea of going with Edward had but just occurred to her.

"Well, dear, there really was not time to arrange that," Elsie said embracing her with motherly affection. "But come now and get some breakfast. You must be hungry after your ride."

"Is Grandpa vexed because I was not here on time?" Zoe asked, following her mother-in-law on her way to the breakfast room.

"He has not shown any vexation," Elsie answered lightly. "You are not much behind time. They are all still at the table. Edward took his breakfast early in order to catch his train."

Zoe's apprehensions were relieved immediately upon entering the breakfast room, as Mr. Dinsmore and all the others greeted her with the usual and pleasant, "Good morning."

Reconciled to her husband and smiled upon by all the rest of the family, she grew quite happy.

In saying she was not to be driven, but would do anything for love and coaxing, she had spoken truly. And now her one great desire was to do something to please Edward.

She had been rather remiss in her studies of late. Though he had administered no reproof, she knew that he felt discouraged over it. She determined to surprise him on his return with her lessons carefully prepared.

After giving due attention to her lessons, she spent hours at the piano learning a song he admired and had lately bought for her. When he had given it to her, he said that he thought it suited her voice and that he wanted to hear her play and sing it.

"What a dear, industrious little woman," Elsie said, meeting her in the hall as she left the music room. Bestowing upon her a motherly smile and caress, she said, "I know whom you are trying so hard to please, and if he does not show appreciation of your efforts, I shall think him unworthy of so good a little wife."

Zoe colored with pleasure. "Oh, mamma," she said, "though I have been cross and willful sometimes, I would do anything in the world to please my husband when he is loving and kind to me. But do you know, I can't bear to be driven. I won't. If anybody tries it with me, it just rouses all that is evil in me."

"Well, dear, I don't think anyone in this house wants to drive you," Elsie said, repeating her caress. "Not even your husband; though he is, perhaps, a trifle masterful by nature. You and he will need to take the two bears into your counsels," she added sportively.

"Two bears, mamma?" Zoe looked up in both surprise and perplexity.

"Yes, dear—bear and forbear—as the poet sings:

> *The kindest and the happiest pair*
> *Will find occasion to forbear,*
> *And something every day they live*
> *To pity and perhaps forgive."*

Zoe went slowly up to her own rooms and sat down to meditate upon her mother-in-law's words.

"'Bear and forbear.' Well, when Edward reproves me as if he were my father instead of my husband and talks about what he will and won't allow, I must bear with him, I suppose. And when I want to answer back that I'm my own mistress and not under his control, I must forbear and deny myself the pleasure. Hard for me to do, but then it isn't to be all on one side. If he will only forbear lecturing me in the beginning, all will go right.

"I mean to tell him so. If he wants me to be very good, he should set me the example. Good! And when he scolds me again, I'll just remind him that example is better than precept. No, I won't either; I'll forbear. Ned is very good to me, and I don't want to provoke him. I mean to be a good little wife to him, and I know he wants to be the best of husbands to me.

"Oh, how kind and good he was to me when papa died and I hadn't another friend in the world! How he took me to his heart and comforted and loved me! I must never make him wish he hadn't. I'll do everything I can to prove that I'm not ungrateful for all his love and kindness."

Tears sprang to her eyes, and she was seized with a longing desire for his presence—for an opportunity to pour out her love and gratitude, and have him clasp her to his heart with the tenderest caresses as was his wont.

She glanced at the clock. Oh, joy! He might, he probably would, return in an hour or perhaps even a trifle sooner.

She sprang up and began dressing for the evening, paying close attention to his taste in the arrangement of her hair and the selection of her dress and ornaments.

"I want to look just as beautiful in his sight as I possibly can, that he may be pleased with me and love me better than ever," was the thought in her heart. "I am his own wife and who has a better right to his love than I? Dear Ned! I hope we'll never quarrel, but always keep the two bears with us in our home."

Her labor completed, she turned herself about before the looking glass and mentally pronounced her attire faultless from the knot of the ribbon in her hair to the dainty boots on the shapely little feet.

Her cheek flushed with pleasure as the mirror told her that face and form were even prettier than the dress and ornaments that formed a fit setting to their charms.

The hour was almost up. She glanced from the window to see if he were yet in sight.

He was not, but she wanted a walk, so would go to meet him. He would dismount at sight of her and they could walk home together.

Tying on a garden hat and throwing a light shawl about her shoulders, she hastened downstairs and out into the grounds.

She had walked more than half the length of the avenue, when she saw the family carriage turning in at the gates, Edward riding beside it.

The flutter of a veil from its window caused her to change her plans. He was not returning alone, but bringing lady visitors. Therefore, she would not go to meet him.

And no one had told her visitors were expected. She felt surprised, and somehow, unreasonable as she knew it to be, she was angry at Edward's look of interest and pleasure as he leaned from the saddle in a listening attitude, as if hearkening to the talk of someone within the carriage.

Zoe had stepped behind a clump of bushes, whose leafy screen hid her from the view of the approaching party, while through its open spaces she could see them very plainly.

As they drew nearer, she saw that the carriage contained two young, pretty, ladylike girls, one of whom was talking to Edward with much animation and earnestness, he listening with evident interest and amusement.

When the carriage had passed her, Zoe glided away through the shrubbery, gained the house by a circuitous route and a side entrance and her own rooms by a back stairway.

She fully expected to find Edward there, but he was not.

"Where can he be?" she asked herself half aloud. Then she sat down and waited for him, but not very patiently.

After some little time, which, to Zoe's impatience, seemed very long, she heard the opening and shutting of a door, then voices of Mr. Dinsmore, his daughter, and Edward in conversation, as they came down the hall together.

"He has been to see his mother first," she pouted. "I think a man ought always to put his wife first." And turning her back to the door, she took up a book and made a pretense of being deeply interested in its perusal.

Edward's step, however, passed on into the dressing room. As she heard him moving about there, she grew more and more vexed. It seemed that he was in no great haste to greet her after their first day's separation. He could put it off, not only for a visit to his mother in her private apartments, but also until he had gone through the somewhat lengthened duties of grooming and getting dressed for supper.

Well, she would show him that she, too, could wait—could be as cool and indifferent as he was. She assumed a graceful attitude in an easy chair, her pretty little feet upon a velvet-cushioned stool. With her book lying in her lap, she listened intently to every sound coming from the adjoining room.

At last she heard his step approach the door, then his hand upon the knob. She instantly took up her book and fixed her eyes upon its open page, as though unconscious of everything but what was printed there, yet really not taking in the meaning of a single word.

Edward came in and was at once close to her side. Still she neither moved nor lifted her eyes. But she could not control her color and so he saw through her pretenses.

He knelt down beside her chair, bent his head, and looked up into her face with laughing eyes.

"What can it be that so interests my little wife that she does not even know that her husband has come home after this first day of separation? Have you no kiss of welcome for him, little woman?"

The book was thrust hastily aside and in an instant her arms were about his neck, her lips pressed again and again to his.

"Oh, Ned, I do love you!" she said softly. "But I began to think you didn't care for me—going to see mamma first, and then waiting to dress."

"Mamma and grandpa were concerned in the business that took me away today, and I owed them a prompt report upon it. Yet, I looked in here first for my wife, but couldn't find her. Then, I asked for her and was told that she had been seen going out for a walk. So I thought I would dress and be ready for her when she came in."

"Was that it?" she asked, looking a little ashamed. "But," regarding him with critical eye, "you'd better always let me help with your dressing. Your cravat isn't tied nicely, and your hair doesn't look half so well as when I brush it for you."

"Can't you set matters straight, then?" he asked, releasing her from the close embrace in which he had held her for the last few minutes.

"Yes, just keep still as you are and I'll retie your cravat, sir."

He held still, enjoying, as he always did, having her deft fingers at work about him, as he gazed all the while into the pretty face with eyes full of loving admiration.

"There!" she said at length, leaning back a little to take in the full effect. "I don't believe that can be improved upon."

"Much obliged," he said, getting up from his knees. "Now, what's next?"

"Your hair, of course," she answered, jumping up and leading the way into the dressing room. "Sit down." Arming herself with comb and brush, "You know I'm not tall enough to reach your head while you're standing up."

He obeyed, asking as he did so, "What have you been doing today?"

"What a question!" she returned laughing. "Of course, I'd take my pleasure when my lord and master was away."

"Please, don't call me that, dear," he said in a tone of gentle, remorseful expostulation.

"Why not? Doesn't the Bible say Sarah obeyed Abraham, calling him lord?"

"But it doesn't say master, and besides, these are very different times."

"We seemed to have changed sides on this subject, somehow," she said with a merry little laugh. She laid the brush away, stood behind his chair, put her arms around his neck, and laid her cheek softly upon his.

He drew her round to a seat upon his knee. "Darling, I don't mean to play the tyrant and am quite ashamed of some things I said last night."

"Then you won't say them any more, will you? I was really afraid you were turning into a horrid tyrant. Oh, Ned, you haven't told me who the visitors are who came in the carriage with you!"

"The daughter and niece of an old friend of my father's, namely Miss Fanny Deane and Miss Susie Fleming."

"How long are they likely to stay?"

"I don't know—probably two or three weeks."

"You asked what I'd been doing. Studying hard part of the time, that I might please this old tutor of mine," she said, giving him another hug. "Will you be pleased to hear me recite now?"

"There would not be time before tea, dear," he said, consulting his watch. "So we will put it off till later in the evening. Come down to the drawing room with me and let me introduce you to our lady visitors."

"Very well, but first tell me if my dress satisfies you, dear."

He gave her a scrutinizing glance. "Entirely—you are as lovely as a little fairy," he said with a proud, fond smile.

"Oh, you flatterer!" she returned with a pleased laugh, slipping her hand into his.

"Your wife!" exclaimed both ladies when the introduction was over. "She looks so young!"

"So very young that I should have taken her for a school girl," added Miss Deane, with a condescending smile that enraged Zoe.

And I take you for an old maid of twenty-five, was her mental retort. I daresay you'd be glad enough to be as young as I am, and to have such a handsome husband. But she merely made a demure little curtsy and withdrew to a seat beside her mother-in-law on the farther side of the room, her heightened color and flashing eyes alone telling how indignant she felt.

"Never mind, dear, you are growing older every day," Elsie said in a soothing undertone. "And you are just the right age for Edward. We all think that, and I think you are a dear, little daughter for me."

"Thank you, dear mamma," whispered Zoe. "I think it was very rude and unkind to liken me to a school girl. I believe it was just because she envies my youth and my husband."

"Perhaps so," Elsie said with difficulty restraining a smile. "But we will try to be charitable and think the remark was not unkindly meant."

Edward took Miss Deane in to supper, which was presently announced. Zoe did not like that fact as Elsie perceived with some concern.

The young lady had very fine conversational powers and was very fond of displaying them. She soon obtained and held the attention of all the older people at the table and Zoe felt herself more and more aggrieved. Edward was positively careless of her wants, leaving her to be waited upon by the servants.

When they returned to the drawing room, he seated himself beside Miss Deane again, and the flow of talk recommenced, as he continued a delighted listener.

Zoe feigned not to notice or care, but it was a very transparent pretense. Edward had devoted himself so almost exclusively to her ever since their marriage that she could scarce endure to have it otherwise.

She could not refrain from watching him furtively and trying to catch his every look, word, and tone.

After a little while, she stole quietly from the room and went up to her own.

"He will miss me presently," she thought, "remember about the lessons, and come up to hear them. And I'll have him all to myself for at least a little while."

He did not come, but at length Rosie looked in to say, "Won't you come down to the music room, Zoe? Miss Fleming is going to play for us, and she is said to be quite a wonderful performer."

Zoe accepted the invitation. She was fond of music and it wasn't Miss Fleming who had robbed her of Edward. Yet, when she saw him standing beside her, a rapt and delighted listener assiduously turning her music, she began to almost hate her, too.

The advent of these strangers seemed to have rendered ineffectual the efforts she had put forth that day to gratify her husband. Of what use was it that she had so carefully prepared lessons he would not trouble himself to hear? Or that she had spent hours of patient practice at the piano in learning the song she was given no opportunity to play and sing?

But womanly pride was awaking within her and she made a tolerably successful effort to control and hide her feelings.

When at length she found herself alone with Edward in their own apartments, she moved silently about making her preparations for retiring, seeming to have nothing to say.

He burst into enthusiastic praise of the talents of their guests—the conversational gift of the one, the musical genius of the other.

Zoe, standing before the mirror, brushing out her soft, shining tresses, made no response.

"Why are you so silent, little woman?" Edward asked presently.

"Because I have nothing to say that you would want to hear."

"Nothing that I would want to hear? Why, I am fond of the very sound of your voice. But whatever is the matter?" for he had come to her side and perceived with surprise and concern that her eyes were full of tears.

"Oh, nothing! Except that I'd looked forward to a delightful evening with my husband, after being parted from him all day, and didn't get it."

"My dear Zoe," he said, "I owe you an apology! I actually forgot all about those lessons."

"And me, too," she said bitterly. "Apparently, my musical and conversational gifts sink into utter insignificance beside those of these new-comers."

"Jealousy is a very mean and wicked passion, Zoe. I don't like to see you indulging it," he said turning away from her. "I am, of course, expected to pay some attention to my mother's guests and you will have to put up with it."

"You are always right and I am always wrong," she said, half choking with indignation. "But if you are always to do as you please, then I shall do as I please, as well."

"In regard to what?" he asked coldly.

"Everything!" she answered in a defiant tone.

Edward strode angrily into the next room. But five minutes sufficed to subdue his passion, and in tender tones he called softly to his wife, "Zoe, love, will you please come here for a moment?"

She started with surprise at the kindness of his tones. Her heart leaped for joy and she ran to him, smiling through her tears.

He had seated himself in a large, easy chair. "Come, darling," he said, drawing her to a seat upon his knee. Then, with his arm about her waist, "Zoe, love, we are husband and wife—nothing but death can ever separate us. Let us be kind to one another, kind and forbearing, so that when one is taken the other will have no cause whatever for self-reproach."

"Oh, Ned, don't talk of that," she sobbed with her arms about his neck, her cheek laid to his. "I'm sure it would kill me to lose you. You are all I have in the wide world."

"So I am, you poor little dear," he said, softly smoothing her hair. "And I ought to be always kind to you. But, indeed, Zoe, you have no need to be jealous of any other woman. I may like to talk with them and listen to their music, but when I want someone to love and cherish, my heart turns to my own little wife."

"It was very foolish!" she said penitently. "But I did so want you to myself tonight, and I'd worked so busily all day learning the lessons and that song you brought me, hoping to please you."

"Did you, dear? Well it was too bad of me to neglect you so and even to forget to give you this, which I bought expressly for my dear, little wife while in the city today."

He took her hand as he spoke and slipped a ring upon her finger.

"Oh, Ned, thank you!" she exclaimed, lifting to his a face full of delight. "It's very pretty and so good of you to remember to bring me something."

"Then, shall we kiss and be friends and try not to quarrel any more?"

"Yes, oh, yes!" she said, offering her lips.

"I must have you perform your song tomorrow," he said caressing her again and again.

"No, no! I can't even think of singing before such a performer as Miss Fleming."

"But you are an early bird, Zoe, and she and Miss Deane will probably lie late. Can't you sing and play for me before they come down in the early morning hours?"

"Well, perhaps," she answered coquettishly. "And the lessons? Will you hear them, too, before breakfast, Ned?"

"If you wish it, dear."

Chapter Seventeenth

*The beginning of strife is as when
one letteth out water: therefore,
leave off contention, before it be meddled with.*

—PROVERBS 17:14

Zoe went to bed that night and rose again the next morning a happy little woman.

Her song was sung, the performance eliciting warm praise from the solitary listener.

Then they had a delightful ride together, all before breakfast. She brought to the table such dancing eyes and rosy cheeks that Mr. Lilburn could not refrain from complimenting her upon them, while the rest of the older people smiled in obvious approval.

"She looks younger than ever," remarked Miss Deane sweetly. "It is quite impossible to realize that she is married."

"It is altogether possible for me to realize that she is my own dear little wife," said Edward, regarding Zoe with loving, admiring eyes. "A piece of personal property I would not part with for untold gold," he added with a happy laugh.

"And we all think Zoe is quite old enough for so young a husband," said Elsie, bestowing upon the two a glance of smiling, motherly affection.

It was a busy season with Edward, and he was compelled to leave the entertainment of the guests throughout the day to his mother and other members of the family.

Zoe excused herself from any share in that work on the plea that she was too young to be companionable to the ladies and spent some hours in diligent study, then walked out with the children.

"I have two sets of lessons ready for you," was her greeting to Edward when he came into their apartments late in the afternoon.

"Have you, my dear?" he returned, taking the easy chair she drew forward for him. "Then, let me hear them. You must have been an industrious, little woman today."

"Tolerably, but you know one set was ready for you yesterday."

"Ah, yes, you were industrious then, also. And I dare say it is rather awful work to study alone."

"Not when one has such a nice teacher," she added sportively. "Praise from your lips is sweeter than it ever was from any other but papa's," she added, tears trembling in her eyes.

He was glad to be able, on the conclusion of the recitation, to give it without stint.

She flushed with great pleasure and helped herself to a seat upon his knee, thanking him with a hug and a kiss.

"Easter holidays begin next week," he remarked, putting an arm about her and returning her caress. "Do you wish to give up your studies during that time, my little wife?"

"No," she said. "I've wasted too much time during the past few weeks and I'd rather take my holidays in the very warm weather."

"That is what mamma's and grandpa's pupils are to do," he said. "They are invited to both the Oaks and the Laurels in May and June to spend some weeks at each place. And you are included in both invitations, Zoe."

"I shall not go unless you do," she said with decision. "Parted from my husband for weeks? No, indeed! I can hardly stand it for a single day," she added, laying her cheek to his.

"Nor I, little wife," he said, passing his hand softly over her hair. "Do you feel equal to a ride this afternoon, darling?"

"Why, yes, of course! Shall I get ready at once?"

"Yes, do, dearie. There is to be a party of us—grandpa, mamma, Miss Fleming, Miss Deane, you, and I."

Zoe's brow clouded. "Riding three abreast, I suppose. But why did you ask Miss Deane? She'll spoil all my enjoyment."

"Don't let her. I must show some attention to her as a guest in the house and really felt obliged to invite her. We are to call at Fairview to see how Lester and Elsie are getting on with their housekeeping. Now, do promise me that you will be a good, sensible, little woman and not indulge in any petty jealousy."

"To please you, I'll do the very best I can. I told you I would do anything for love and coaxing," she answered in a sprightly tone, with her arm still about his neck, her eyes gazing fondly into his.

He drew her closer. "I'll try always to remember and practice upon that," he said. "Now, darling, I would be very pleased if you would don that very becoming hat and habit you wore this morning."

Miss Deane was an accomplished coquette, whose greatest delight was to prove her power over every man who came in her way, whether married or single. Perceiving Zoe's dislike of her and jealousy of any attention paid her by Edward, she took a malicious pleasure in drawing him to her side whenever opportunity offered and keeping him there as long as possible.

Edward, with a heart entirely true to his young wife, endeavored to resist the fascinations of the siren and avoid her when politeness would permit. And Zoe struggled against her inclination to jealousy, yet Miss Deane succeeded in the course of a few days in bringing about a slight coldness between the lovers.

They did not actually quarrel, but there was a cessation of loving looks and endearing words and names. It was simply Zoe and Edward now instead of dearest and love and darling, while they rather avoided than sought each other's company.

Edward was too busy to walk or ride with his wife, and Max and Ralph Conley—at home now for the Easter holidays and self-invited to Ion—became the almost constant sharers of her outdoor exercise.

Edward saw it with displeasure, for Ralph was no favorite of his. When things had gone on in that way for several days, he ventured upon a mild remonstrance, telling Zoe he would rather she would not make a familiar associate of Ralph.

"Well, if I am constantly denied my husband's company, I simply will not be blamed for taking whatever company I can get," she answered coldly.

"I don't blame you for what is past, Zoe," he said. "But I do request that in the future you will not have more to do with Ralph than is quite necessary for politeness' sake."

Zoe was in a defiant mood. She walked away without making any reply, and an hour later Edward met her riding out with Ralph by her side. Max was not with them as it was during his study hours, and they had not even an attendant.

They had been laughing and chatting merrily, but at the sight of Edward a sudden silence fell upon the two of them.

Zoe's head drooped and her cheeks flushed hotly as she perceived the dark frown on her husband's brow. She expected some cutting word of rebuke, but he simply wheeled his horse about, placed himself on her other side, so that she was between him and Ralph, and rode on with them.

Not a word was spoken until they drew rein at their own door, when Edward, dismounting, lifted his wife from her pony. As he sat her down, he said, "I will be obliged to you, Zoe, if you will go now to prepare your lessons for today."

Zoe had already begun to repent of her open disregard for his wishes, for during the silent ride, her memory had been busy with the many expressions of love and tenderness he had lavished upon her in their short married life. If there had been the least bit of either in his tones now, she would have whispered in his ear that she was sorry and would not so offend again. But, the cold, stern accents made the request sound like a command and roused again the spirit of opposition that had almost died out.

She shook off his detaining hand and walked away in silence with head erect and cheeks burning with indignation.

Ralph had not heard Edward's low spoken words, but looking after Zoe as she disappeared within the doorway, "Seems to me you're a bit of a tyrant, Ned," he remarked with his usual, coarse, disagreeable laugh.

"I'm not aware of having shown any evidence of being such," Edward returned rather haughtily as he remounted. Then, turning his horse's head, he rode rapidly away.

Zoe went to her boudoir, gave vent to her anger in a hearty fit of crying, then set to work at the lessons with a sincere desire to please the husband she really loved with all her heart.

"I've been forgetting the two bears," she said to herself. "But I'll try again. When that hateful Miss Deane goes away, everything will be right again. I know Ned has to be polite to her, but I can't help being jealous, because he's my all in all."

She finished her tasks, dressed herself for dinner with care and taste, and when she heard his step on the stairs ran to the door to meet him.

Her face was bright and eager but changed at the sight of his cold, forbidding look.

"I am ready for you," she said timidly, shrinking away from him.

"Very well, bring your books," he said with, she thought, the air of a schoolmaster toward a pupil in disgrace, seating himself as he spoke.

She brought them, keeping her eyes cast down to hide the telltale tears. She controlled her emotion in another moment and went through her recitations very creditably, she thought.

Edward made no comment upon them, where usually he would have bestowed warm praise. He simply appointed the tasks for the next day, rose, and left the room.

Zoe looked after him with a swelling heart, wiped away a tear or two, and assuming an air of indifference, went down to the parlor to join the rest of the family.

"Where's Ned?" asked Rosie. "You two used to never be seen apart, but of late—"

The sentence was suddenly broken off because of a warning look from her mamma.

"Don't you know, little girl," said Miss Deane in a soft purring tone, "that nobody expects married people to remain lovers always?"

"It is what they should do," Elsie said with gentle decision. "It was so with my husband and myself, and I trust will be with all my children."

"Allow me to advise you to deliver Ned a lecture on the subject, cousin," laughed Ralph.

"He doesn't need it," Zoe exclaimed with spirit, turning on Ralph with flashing eyes.

"Oh," he said, with a loud guffaw, "I should have remembered that anyone taking on the part of an abused wife is sure to have her wrath turned upon himself."

"What do you mean by that, sir? I am not an abused wife," said Zoe, tears springing to her eyes. "There never was a kinder, more tender husband than mine, and I know he loves me dearly."

"He does indeed, dear. We, none of us, doubt that in the least. So you can well afford to let Ralph enjoy his forlorn joke," remarked Mrs. Dinsmore, with an indignant, reproving look at the latter, who colored under it and lapsed into silence.

The weather was delightful and the children, having been given a half holiday, spent the afternoon on the grounds. Zoe forsook the company of the older people for theirs and joined in their sports, for she was still childlike in her tastes.

She was as active as a boy and before her marriage had taken keen delight in climbing rocks and trees. The apple trees in the orchard were in full bloom. Taking a fancy to adorn herself with their blossoms, she climbed up among the branches of one of the tallest in order, as she said, to "take her pick and choice." Rosie, Lulu, Gracie, and Walter were standing near watching her with eager interest.

"Oh, Zoe, do take care!" Rosie called to her. "That branch doesn't look strong enough to hold you, and you might fall and hurt yourself badly."

"Don't be afraid. I can take care of myself," she returned with a light laugh.

But another voice spoke close at hand fairly startling her, it was so unexpected. "Zoe, what mad prank is this? Let me help you down at once."

"There's no need for you to trouble yourself. I am quite able to get down without assistance when I'm ready," she replied, putting a strong emphasis upon the last words.

"No, it is too dangerous." And he held up his arms with an imperative, "Come!"

"How dare you order me about, Edward," she muttered under her breath and was quite inclined to rebel.

But, no; the children were looking and listening to every word, and they must not be allowed to suspect any unpleasantness between herself and her husband.

She dropped into his arms. He set her upon her feet, drew her hand within his arm, and walked away with her.

"I do not approve of tree climbing for a married woman, Zoe," he said, when they were out of earshot of the children. "At least, not for my wife. And I must request that you not try it again."

"It's a pity I didn't know how much my liberty would be curtailed by getting married," she returned bitterly.

"And I am exceedingly sorry it is out of my power to restore your liberty to you, since it seems that would add to your happiness."

At that she hastily withdrew her hand from his arm and walked quickly away from him, taking the direction of the house.

Leaning against a tree, his arms folded, his face pale and stern, he looked after her with a heart full of keenest anguish. She had never been dearer to him than at that moment, but alas, she seemed to have lost her love for him. What a life of miserable dissension they were likely to lead, repenting at leisure their foolishly hasty marriage!

She was frantic with pain and passion as well. He was tired of her already—before they had been married a year—he did not love her any longer and would be glad to be rid of her. Oh, what should she do! Would that she could fly to the ends of the earth that he might be relieved of her hated presence.

And yet—oh, how could she ever endure any absence from him? She loved him so dearly, so very dearly!

She hurried on past the house, down the whole length of the avenue and back again, the hot tears all the time streaming over her cheeks. Then she hastily wiped them away, went to her rooms, bathed her eyes, and dressed carefully for tea.

Womanly pride had come to her aid. She must hide her wounds from all, especially from Edward himself and "that detestable Miss Deane." She would pretend to be happy—so very, very happy, and no one should guess how terribly her heart was aching.

Chapter Eighteenth

Where lives the man that has not tried
How mirth can into folly glide,
And folly into sin!

—Scott

Ralph Conly was not a favorite with any of his Ion relatives because they knew his principles were not altogether such as they could approve, nor indeed his practice either. Yet, they had no idea how bad a youth he actually was, or else intimacy between him and Max would have been forbidden.

All unsuspected by the older people, he was exerting a very demoralizing influence over the younger boy. Every afternoon they sought out some private spot and had a game of cards, and little by little Ralph had introduced gambling into the game, till now the stakes were high in proportion to the means of the players.

On this particular afternoon they had taken possession of a summer-house in a retired part of the grounds and were deep in play.

Ralph at first let Max win, the stakes being very small. Then, raising them higher, he won again and again, till he had stripped Max of all his pocket money and his watch.

Max felt himself absolutely ruined and broke out in passionate exclamations of both grief and despair, coupled with accusations of cheating. These accusations were, indeed, well founded.

Ralph grew furious and swore horrible oaths, and Max answered with a repetition of his accusation, concluding with an oath—the first he had uttered since his father's serious talk with him on the exceeding sinfulness and black ingratitude of the use of profanity.

All that had passed then—the passage of Scripture telling of the punishment of the swearer under the Levitical law—flashed back upon him as the words left his lips. And so, covering his face with his hands, he groaned in an anguish of spirit at the thought of his terrible sin.

Then Mr. Dinsmore's voice, speaking in sternest accents, startled them both. "Ralph, is this the kind of boy you are? A gambler and profane swearer? And you, too, Max? Do you mean to break your poor father's heart and someday bring down his grey hairs with sorrow to the grave? Go at once to your room, sir. And you, Ralph, return immediately to Roselands. I cannot and will not expose my grandchildren to the corrupting influence of such a character as yours."

The mandate was obeyed promptly and in silence by both. Ralph did not even dare to gather up his plunder or his cards from the table where they lay.

Mr. Dinsmore took possession of both and followed Max to the house. In the heat of their altercation the lads had raised their voices to a high pitch. Mr. Dinsmore, happening to be at no great distance, hastened to the spot to learn the cause of the great disturbance and had come upon them in time to hear the last sentence uttered by each. He had taken in the whole situation at a glance.

Horace went directly to his daughter's dressing room and sent for Violet to join them there.

Both ladies were greatly distressed by the tale he had to tell.

"Oh," sobbed Violet, "it will break my husband's heart to learn that his only son has taken to such evil courses! And to think that it was a relative of our own who led him into it!"

"Yes," sighed Mr. Dinsmore. "I blame myself for not being more watchful. I had no idea that Ralph had acquired such vices."

"I cannot have you blame yourself, papa," Elsie said with tender look and tone. "I am sure it was no fault of yours. And I cannot believe the dear boy has become a confirmed swearer or gambler in so short a time. He is a warm-hearted fellow and has a tender conscience. We will hope by divine aid to reclaim him speedily."

"Dear mamma, thank you!" exclaimed Violet, smiling through her tears. "What you say of Max is quite true, and I have no doubt that he is at this very moment greatly distressed because of his sin."

"I trust it may be so," said Mr. Dinsmore. "But now the question is, what is to be done with him? I wish his father were here to prescribe the course to be taken."

"Oh, but he has already done so!" cried Violet, bursting into tears again. "He said if Max should ever be guilty of profanity he was to be confined to his room for a week and forbidden communication with the rest of the family as unworthy to associate with them. I begged him not to compel us to be so severe, but he was inexorable."

"Then we have no discretionary power, no choice but to carry out his directions," Mr. Dinsmore said, feeling rather relieved that the decision was not left to him. "I shall go now and tell Max what his sentence is, and from whom it comes.

"And, unfortunately, it will be necessary, in order to carry it out, to inform the other members of the family, who might otherwise hold communication with him. That unpleasant task I leave to you, Elsie and Violet."

He left the room, and Violet, after a little sorrowful converse with her mother, went to her own. With many tears she told Lulu and Gracie what had occurred, and what was, by their father's direction, to be Max's punishment.

Both little sisters were shocked, grieved, and very sorry for Max—for it seemed to them quite terrible to be shut up in one room for a whole week, while to be out of doors was so delightful.

But even Lulu had nothing to say against their father's decree, especially after Violet had explained that he had made it in his great love for Max. Their father wanted to cure him of vices that would make him wretched in this life and the next.

Rosie was still more shocked and scarcely less sorry than Lulu and Gracie, for she had been taught to look upon swearing and gambling as very great sins. Yet she liked Max very much indeed and pitied him for the disgrace and punishment he had brought upon himself.

It was Rosie who told Zoe, seeking her out in her dressing room where she was getting dressed for the evening.

"Oh, Rosie, how dreadful!" exclaimed Zoe. "I never could have believed it of Max! But it is all because of the bad influence of that wicked Ralph. I see now why Edward disapproves of him so thoroughly that he didn't like me to ride with him. But I do think Captain Raymond is a very severe father. A whole week in the house in this lovely weather! How can the poor boy ever stand it? And nobody to speak a kind word to him, either. I don't think they ought to be so hard on him, for I dare say he is grieving himself sick over it now, for he isn't a bad boy."

"No," said Rosie, "I don't think he is. I like Max very much, but of course his father's orders have to be carried out. For that reason we are all forbidden to go near him and we have no choice but to obey."

"Forbidden, indeed!" thought Zoe to herself. "I for one shall do as I please about it."

"Zoe, how pretty you are! That dress is very becoming!" exclaimed Rosie, suddenly changing the subject.

"Am I? But I can't compare with Miss Deane in either beauty or conversational powers," returned Zoe, the concluding words spoken with more than a little bitterness.

"Can't you? Just ask Ned about it," laughed Rosie. "I verily believe he thinks you the sweetest thing he ever set eyes on. There, I hear him coming and must run away—for I know he always wants you to himself here, and, besides, I have to dress."

She ran merrily away, passing her older brother on the threshold.

Zoe had made herself busy frantically searching for something and did not look toward him or speak. In another moment, she had found what she wanted, closed the drawer, and passed into her boudoir.

Edward had been standing there silently watching her, love and anger struggling for the mastery in his heart. If she had only turned to him with a word, or even a look of regret for the past, and desire for reconciliation, he would have taken her to his heart again as fully and tenderly as ever. He was longing to do so, but too proud to make the first advances when he felt himself the aggrieved one.

"All would be right between them but for Zoe's silly jealousy and pride. Why could she not trust him and submit willingly to his guidance and control while she was still so young and inexperienced—such a mere child as to be incapable of judging for herself in any matter of importance? In fact, he felt it his duty to guide her till she should grow older and wiser."

Such were his thoughts as he went through the duties of dressing. Meanwhile Zoe sat at the window of her boudoir gazing out over the smoothly shaven lawn with its stately trees, lovely in their fresh spring attire, to the green field and woods beyond. Yet she could scarcely take in the beauty of the landscape, so full of tears were her eyes—so full of anger, grief, and pain was her heart.

She had not even looked at her husband as he stood silently near her a moment ago, but she felt that he had been gazing with anger and sternness upon her.

"If he had only said one kind word to me," she whispered to herself. "I would have told him I was sorry for my silly speech this afternoon and oh, so happy to be his own little wife. That is, if—if only he hasn't quit loving me."

She hastily wiped her eyes and endeavored to assume an air of cheerfulness and indifference as she heard his steps approaching.

"Are you ready to go down now, Zoe?" he asked in a freezing tone.

"Yes," she answered, turning to follow him as he led the way to the door.

There seemed to be a tacit understanding between them that their disagreements and coldness toward each other were to be concealed from all the rest of the world. In happier days, they had always gone down together to the drawing room or the tea table; therefore, they would do so still.

Also, they studiously guarded their words and looks in the presence of any third person.

Yet Elsie, the tender mother, with eyes sharpened by affection, had already perceived that all was not right. She had noted Zoe's disturbed look when Edward seemed specially interested in Miss Deane's talk or Miss Fleming's music and had silently determined not to ask them to prolong their stay at Ion.

The supper bell rang as Edward and Zoe descended the stairs together, and they immediately obeyed its summons without going into the drawing room.

Violet's place at the table was vacant as was that of Max, and Lulu and Gracie bore the traces of tears about their eyes.

These things reminded Zoe of Max's trouble, forgotten for a time in her own, and she thought pityingly of him in his imprisonment. She also wondered if he would be put upon prison fare and determined to find out. She then decided that if he were, she would try to procure him something better.

She made an errand to her own room soon after leaving the table, went to his door, and knocked very softly.

"Who's there?" he asked in a voice choked up with sobs.

"It is I, Maxie," she said in an undertone at the keyhole. "Zoe, you know. I want to say I'm ever so sorry for you and always ready to do anything I can to help you."

"Thank you," he said. "But I must not see anybody, so can't open the door. Indeed," he said with a heavy sob, "I'm not fit company for you or any of the rest."

"Yes, you are. You're as good as I am. But why can't you open the door? Are you locked in?"

"No, but—papa said I—I must stay by myself for a week if—if I did what I have done today. So please don't stay any longer, though it was ever so good of you to come."

"Goodbye, then," and she moved silently away.

Chapter Nineteenth

High minds of native pride and force
Most deeply feel thy pangs, remorse!
Fear of their scourge mean villains have;
Thou art the torture of the brave.

—Scott

*M*ax sat before his writing table, his folded arms upon it, and his face hidden upon them. He was in sore distress of mind. How he had fallen before temptation! Into what depths of disgrace and sin! Sin that in olden times would have been punished with death, even as the horrible crime of murder. How that must still be as hateful as ever in the sight of an unchangeable God.

And not only that sin, of which he had thought he had so truly and deeply repented, but another that he had always been taught was a very low and degrading vice. Oh, could there actually be forgiveness for him?

And how would his dear, honored father feel when the sad story should reach his ears? Would it indeed break his heart as Grandpa Dinsmore had said? The boy's own heart was overwhelmed with grief, dismay, and remorse as he asked himself these and other torturing questions one upon the other over and over again.

The door opened, but so softly that the sound was lost in his bitter sobbing. Then a hand rested lightly, tenderly upon his bowed head and a gentle, pitying voice said, "My poor, dear boy, my heart bleeds for you."

"Oh, Grandma Elsie!" he burst out. "Can you say that to such a wicked fellow as I am?"

"Did Jesus weep with compassion over the sinners of Jerusalem, many of whom were even then plotting His death? And, Maxie, He pities you in your fallen estate and is ready to forgive you the moment you turn to Him with grief and hatred of your sin and an earnest desire to forsake it and to give yourself to His service."

"Oh, I do hate it!" he cried out with vehemence. "I didn't mean ever to swear any more, and I feel as if I'd rather cut off my right hand than to do it again! But oh, how can I ask Him to forgive me, when He did once, now I've gone and done the same wicked thing again, just as if I hadn't really been sorry at all, though I was sure I was? Grandma Elsie, what shall I do?"

"'Let the wicked forsake his way, and the unrighteous man his thoughts; let him return unto the Lord, and He will abundantly pardon.'

"'He is the Lord, the Lord God, merciful and gracious, longsuffering and abundant in goodness and truth, keeping mercy for thousands, forgiving iniquity and transgression and sin.'

"'His name is Jesus, for He shall save His people from their sins.' He says, 'Him that cometh to Me, I will in no wise cast out.' 'O Israel, thou hast destroyed thyself; but in Me is thine help.'

"'Though your sins be as scarlet, they shall be as white as snow; though they be red like crimson, they shall be as wool.'

"'I, even I, am He that blotteth out thy transgressions for my own sake, and will not remember thy sins.'"

"Oh, He is very good to say that!" sobbed the penitent boy. "But won't you ask Him to forgive me, Grandma Elsie?"

"Yes, Max, but you must pray, too, for yourself. Confess your sins to Him and ask Him to blot them out and remember them no more against you, because Jesus has suffered their penalty in your stead. Shall we kneel down right now and ask Him together?"

She stayed with him some time longer, talking in tender, motherly fashion—not extenuating his guilt, but speaking of the blood that cleanseth from all sin, the love and tender compassion of Jesus, His willingness and ability to save them to the uttermost that come unto God by Him.

She warned him, too, of the danger of evil associates and from indulgence in the vice of gambling.

Then she told him he was not too young to begin to lead a Christian life and urged him to do so without a moment's delay.

"I think I do want to be a Christian, Grandma Elsie," he said. "If I only knew how."

"It is to leave the service of Satan for that of the Lord Jesus Christ," she said. "It is to give yourself body and soul, at once and forever, to Jesus, trusting Him alone for your salvation from sin and eternal death.

"'Believe on the Lord Jesus Christ, and thou shalt be saved.' 'Look unto Me and be ye saved, all the ends of the earth.'

"Just take the first step, Max, and He will help you on all the way, one step at a time, till you reach the gates of the celestial city. 'This God is our God forever and ever, He will be our guide even unto death.'

"Just speak to the Lord Jesus, dear Max, as if you could see Him standing before you while you knelt at His feet. Say to Him as the leper did, 'Lord, if Thou wilt, Thou canst make me clean.' Tell Him how full you are of the dreadful leprosy of sin, how unable to heal yourself. And beseech Him to do the work for you, to wash you and make you clean and cover you with the robe of His righteousness. Give yourself to Him, asking Him to accept the worthless gift and make you entirely and forever His own."

She rose to leave him.

"Oh, do stay a little longer!" he pleaded, clinging to her hand. "Tell me, do you think Mamma Vi will ever love me any more? That she will ever kiss me again?" he sobbed.

"I am sure she will, Max," Elsie answered in moved tones. "She has not ceased to love you, and I think will come and speak a word to you now, if you wish it."

"Oh, so much! Only—only I'm dreadfully ashamed to look her in the face. And—oh, Grandma Elsie, do you think it will break my father's heart when he hears it all?"

"It will make him very sad indeed, I have no doubt, Max," she answered gently. "But if he hears, too, that you have truly repented and given your heart to God, he cannot fail to be greatly comforted. Tell him the whole truth, my dear boy, and do not try to conceal anything from him."

"It's what I mean to do, Grandma Elsie," he said with a heavy sigh. "Though I'd rather take the worst kind of a flogging. And that's what I'd get if he was here, for he told me so."

"I am very glad you love your father so well, Max, and that your sorrow is more for grieving him and especially for having dishonored and displeased God, than for the unpleasant consequences to yourself. It gives me great hope that you will never be guilty of such conduct again.

"Now, I shall go and send your mamma to you. She is in her own rooms for she has been too much distressed over her dear boy's sad fall to join the others at the table or in the drawing room. She loves you very dearly, Max."

"It's very good of her," he said in trembling tones. "Oh, I'm ever so sorry to have grieved her so!"

Violet was greatly comforted by her mother's report of her talk with Max, because both saw in his conduct and words the evidence of sincere repentance toward God. This evidence giving them strong hope of his future avoidance of the sins of profanity and gambling.

She went to him presently, put her arms about him, kissed him, wept with him, and like her mother, pointed him to the Savior—telling of His willingness to forgive every truly penitent soul.

"Oh, Mamma Vi," he sobbed, "I thought I was that before, when papa showed me what an awful sin swearing was. I didn't think I would ever do it again. But I got dreadfully angry with Ralph because he cheated me out of everything—all my money and my watch that I've always thought so much of, you know—and the wicked words slipped out before I knew it. They just seemed to speak themselves."

"Ah, Max, that is one of the dreadful consequences of allowing ourselves to fall into such wicked ways. It is the power of habit that grows upon us till we are bound by it as with an iron chain. The Bible says, 'His own iniquities shall take the wicked himself, and he shall be holden with the cords of his sins.' So, the longer anyone lives in his sin, the harder it is for him to break away from it—to repent and be converted and saved. Therefore, I beseech you to come to Jesus now; God's time is always now."

"Mamma Vi, I think I have," he said low and humbly. "I tried to do it with my heart when Grandma Elsie was praying for me."

"Oh, Max, dear Max, I am very glad!" she returned with tears of joy in her eyes. "And your father will rejoice almost as the angels do in heaven when a sinner repents and is saved."

"It's a dreadful task to have to write down all about this afternoon for him to read in my diary," sighed the boy.

"But you will do it, Max? Will you tell him the whole truth like the brave boy I know you to be?" queried Violet anxiously.

"Yes, ma'am, I will. Oh, I wish he were here so I could just tell him and have it all over in a few minutes! But now, it will be so long that I'll have to wait to hear what he has to say about it."

Violet expressed her sympathy, joined very heartily in his wish for his father's presence, then left him to his task.

"Seems to me it's a little like marching up to the cannon's mouth," Max said to himself as he took out his writing materials and dipped his pen in the ink. "But it's got to be done, and I'll have it over."

He cogitated a moment, then began. "Dear papa, I've been doing very wrong for 'most a week— letting a fellow teach me to play cards and gamble. We didn't play for money or anything but fun at first, but afterward we did. I lost all the money I had, and, worse still, the nice watch you sent me.

"But the very worst is to come. You would never believe I could be so terribly wicked after all you said to me. And I wouldn't have believed it myself, and oh, I don't like to tell you, for I'm afraid it will almost break your heart, papa, to know you have such a wicked boy for your only son!

"But I have to tell you, because you know you said I must tell you everything bad I did.

"Well, I was sure the fellow had cheated, and I got very mad and called him a cheat and a thief. Then he got mad and swore horrible oaths at me and called me a liar. That made me madder than ever, and—oh, papa, how can I write it for you to see? I swore at him, papa."

The boy's tears were dropping onto the paper. He dashed them hastily away and went on writing.

"I am dreadfully sorry, papa! I think I was never so sorry for anything in all my life, because—because it was so wicked and ungrateful to God. I've asked Him to forgive me for Jesus' sake, and Grandma Elsie has asked Him for me, too, and Mamma Vi told me she had been praying for me. And I've tried to give myself to the dear Savior, and I hope I'll be His servant all the rest of my life.

"I think He has forgiven me, and will you forgive me, too, papa? I'm to stay alone here in my room for a whole week. Mamma Vi says that was the way you had told her I should be punished, if ever I did that wicked thing again, and it isn't a bit worse than I deserve."

Chapter Twentieth

There are that raise up strife and contention.

—Habakkuk 1:3

Only by pride cometh contention.

—Proverbs 13:10

While Zoe was at Max's door, something took Edward to their rooms. He was there but a moment—just long enough to pick up the article he wanted. Hurrying down the hall again, he caught the sound of her voice as he reached the head of the stairway.

For an instant he stood still, debating within himself whether to interfere or not. Deciding in the negative, he passed on down the stairs more angry with her than ever.

She was defying not only his authority, but also that of his grandfather and mother. She was also interfering with their management of the children committed to their care by their own father. Truly, he feared he had made a sad mistake in putting such a child into a woman's position where she felt herself entitled to rights, but for whose proper exercise she quite obviously had not yet sufficient judgment or self-control.

As he entered the drawing room, Miss Deane, who was seated at a table looking over a portfolio of drawings and engravings, called him to her side.

"You have visited these places, Mr. Travilla," she said, "and I would like the benefit of your explanations and your opinion as to whether the pictures are true to nature. They are European views, I see."

Of course he could not, without great rudeness, refuse to take a seat by her side and give her the information she requested.

So it happened that when Zoe came in presently after, her anger was intensely aroused by seeing her husband and Miss Deane seated at a distant table, apart from the rest of the occupants of the room, laughing and talking with their heads very close together over an engraving.

Edward lifted his just in time to catch her look of mingled amazement, scorn, and indignation. He flushed hotly and remembering what he had just overheard upstairs and what had passed between them in the apple orchard, gave her an angry glance in return.

She drew her slight, girlish figure up to its full height and turned away, crossing the room toward a sofa where Mrs. Dinsmore and a bachelor gentleman of the neighborhood sat conversing together.

A sudden impulse seized her as Mr. Larned rose and took her hand in greeting, for at the same moment, Mrs. Dinsmore was called from the room by a servant, who said that someone was waiting in the hall to speak to her.

"I'll pay Edward back in his own coin," Zoe said to herself. Mr. Larned was surprised at the great cordiality and winning sweetness of her manner as she took the vacated seat by his side, then at the spirit and vivacity with which she rattled away to him—now on this theme, now on that.

Excitement lent an unwonted glow to her cheek and a brilliancy and sparkle to her expressive, always-beautiful eyes.

Edward, watching her furtively with darkening brow, thought he had never seen her so pretty and fascinating. Never had her low, soft laugh, as now and again it reached his ear, sounded so silvery sweet and musical, yet it jarred his nerves and he would feign have stopped it.

He hoped momentarily that Mr. Larned would go, but he sat on and on the whole evening, as Zoe entertained him all the while.

Other members of the family came in, but though he rose to greet them, he immediately resumed his seat. She kept hers as well—in spite of the frowning looks her husband gave her from time to time, but which she feigned not to see.

At length, his mother, perceiving with pain what was going on, managed to release him from Miss Deane, and he at once took a seat on his wife's other side and joined in the talk.

Zoe had but little to say after that and Mr. Larned presently took his departure.

That was a signal for the good nights and all the family scattered to their rooms.

Zoe's heart quaked as the door of her boudoir closed upon her, shutting her in alone with her absolutely irate husband.

She knew that he was angry, more angry with her than he had ever been before. And though, in her thoughts, she tried to put all the blame on him, conscience told her that she was by no means blameless in the whole affair.

He locked the door, then turned toward her. She glanced up at him half defiantly, half timidly. His look was very stern and cold.

She turned away with a pout and a slight shrug of her pretty shoulders.

"It seems your smiles are for Miss Deane while your black looks are reserved only for your wife," she said.

"I have no interest in Miss Deane," he replied. "It is nothing to me how she behaves, but my wife's conduct is a matter of vital importance. And, let me tell you, Zoe, I will have no more such exhibitions as you made of yourself tonight with either Mr. Larned or any other man. I won't allow it. There are some things a man won't put up with. You must and shall show some respect to my wishes in regard to this."

"Orders, you'd better say," she muttered.

"Well, then, orders, if you prefer it."

She was also very angry and withal a good deal frightened at the scene.

"Exhibitions indeed!" she cried, sinking into a chair for she was trembling from head to foot. "What did I do? Why had you any more right to laugh and talk with another woman than I another man, Edward?"

"Laughing and talking may be well enough, but it was more than that. You were actually flirting."

"You call it that just because you are jealous. And if I was, it was your fault—setting me the example by flirting with Miss Deane."

"I did nothing of the kind," he returned haughtily. "I sat beside her against my will, simply because she requested me to go over those sketches and engravings with her. I couldn't in politeness refuse."

"Well, I didn't know that, and you needn't scold me for following your example."

"I tell you I did not set you the example. And I advise you to beware how you behave so again. Also, you had better mind how you interfere in the discipline grandpa and mamma see proper to use toward Max and his sisters, as you did tonight."

"So you have been acting the spy upon your wife as well!" she interrupted in scornful indignation.

"No, I overheard you quite accidentally. It is the second time you have done so, and I warn you to let it be the last."

"Indeed! Why don't you say at once that you'll beat me if I don't obey all your tyrannical orders?"

"Because it would not be true, Zoe. Should I ever so far forget myself as to lift my hand against my own wife, I could never again lay claim to the name of gentleman."

"Perhaps, then, you will lock me up?" she sneered.

"Possibly I may, if you make it necessary," he said coldly.

"Lock me up, indeed! I'd like to see you try it!" she cried, starting up with flashing eyes and stamping her foot in a sort of fury of indignation.

Then, rushing into the adjoining room, she tore off her ornaments and dress, pulled down her hair—her cheeks burning, her eyes hot and dry.

But by the time she had assumed her night-gown, the first fury of passion had spent itself and scalding tears were raining down her cheeks.

She threw herself on the bed, sobbing convulsively. "Oh, I never, never thought he would treat me so! And he wouldn't dare if papa was alive. But he knows I've nobody to defend me—nobody in the wide world and he can abuse me as much as he pleases. But I think it's very mean for a big, strong man to be cruel to a little, weak woman."

Then, as her anger cooled still more, "But I have done and said provoking things today as well as he," she acknowledged to herself. "I suppose if I'd been in his place I'd have been mad, too and scolded and threatened my wife. Well, if he'd only come and kiss me and coax me a little, I'd say I was sorry and didn't intend to vex him so any more."

She hushed her sobs and listened. She could hear him moving about in the dressing room.

"Edward!" she called in soft, tremulous tones.

No answer.

She waited a moment, then called a little louder, "Ned!"

Again, there was no reply, and she turned over on her pillow and cried herself to sleep.

When she woke all was darkness and silence.

She felt frightened.

"Edward," she said softly and put out her hand to feel him.

He was not there. She sprang from the bed and groped her way into the dressing room.

There the moon shone in, and by its light she perceived the form of her husband stretched upon a couch, while the sound of his breathing told her that he slept.

She crept back to her bed and lay down upon it with such a sense of utter loneliness as she had never known before.

"Oh," she moaned to herself, "he hates me, he hates me! He wouldn't even lie down beside me! He will never love me any more."

She wept for a long time, but at last fell into a profound sleep.

When she next awakened again, day had dawned, but it was earlier than their usual hour for rising.

The first object that met her sleepy gaze was her husband's untouched pillow and the sight instantly and painfully brought back the events of the previous day and night.

Her first thought was resentment toward her husband, but better thoughts succeeded. She loved him dearly, and for the sake of peace she would humble herself a little. She would go and wake him with a kiss and say she was sorry to have vexed him, and if he'd only be kind and not order her, she wouldn't do so any more.

She slipped out of bed, stole noiselessly to the door of the dressing room, and looked in.

He was not there, and the room was in great disorder—closet and wardrobe doors open and things scattered here and there, as if he had made a hasty selection of garments, tossing aside such as he did not want.

As Zoe gazed about in wonder and surprise, the sound of wheels caught her ear.

She ran to a window overlooking a side entrance and dropped on her knees before it to look and to listen without danger of being seen.

There stood the family carriage. Edward was in the act of handing Miss Fleming into it, Miss Deane followed, and he stepped in after her, only pausing a moment with his foot upon the step to turn and answer a question from his mother.

"How long do you expect to be gone, Edward?" Elsie asked.

"Probably a week or ten days, mother," he replied. "Goodbye," and in another instant the carriage rolled away.

Zoe felt stunned, bewildered, as she knelt there leaning her head against the window-frame and watched till it was out of sight.

"Gone!" she said aloud. "Gone without one word of goodbye to me, without telling me he was going, without saying he was sorry for his cruel words last night, and with Miss Deane. Oh, I know now that he hates me and will never, never love me again!"

Bitter, scalding tears streamed from her eyes. She rose presently and began mechanically picking up and putting away his clothes. She then got dressed for the day, stopping every now and then to wipe away her tears, for she was crying all the time.

The breakfast bell rang at the accustomed hour, but she could not bear the thought of going down and showing her tear-swollen eyes at the table. Besides, she did not feel hungry. She thought she would never want to eat again.

After a little, opening the door in answer to a rap, she found Agnes standing there with a delightful breakfast on a silver tray—hot coffee, delicate rolls and muffins, tender beefsteak, and an omelet.

"Good mornin', Miss Zoe," said the girl, walking in and setting her burden down on a stand. "Miss Elsie she tole me for to fotch up dis yere. She tink, Miss Elsie do, dat p'raps you'd rather eat yo' breakfus up yere dis mornin'."

"Yes, so I would, Agnes. Though I'm not very hungry. Tell mamma she is most kind, and I am much obliged."

"Ya'as, Miss Zoe," Agnes curtsied and withdrew.

Zoe took a sip of the coffee, tasted the omelet, found a coming appetite, and went on to make a tolerably hearty meal, growing more cheerful and hopeful as she ate.

But grief overcame her again as she went about the solitary rooms. It seemed as if her husband's presence lingered everywhere, as if he were dead and buried, and she never to see him more.

Not quite a year had elapsed since her father's death. The scenes of that day and night and many succeeding ones came vividly before her—the utter forlornness of her condition. She had been alone in a strange land with a dying parent and no earthly comforter at hand, no friend or helper in the wide world. How Edward had flown to her assistance, how kindly he had ministered to her dying father, and how tenderly he had taken her in his arms—whispering words of both love and sympathy to her as he asked her to become his wife and give him the right to protect and care for her.

How he had lavished favors and endearments upon her all these months. How patiently he had borne with both petulance and frequent disregard for his known wishes. Nor had he ever once reminded her that she owed her home and every earthly blessing to him.

How he had sympathized with her in her bursts of grief for her father, soothed her with tenderest caresses and assurances of the bliss of the departed, and reminded her of the blessed hope of reunion in the better land.

After all this, she surely might have borne a little from him—a trifling neglect or reproof, a slight exertion of authority, especially as she could not deny that she was very young and foolish to be left to her own guidance.

And perhaps he had a right to claim obedience from her, for she knew in her vows that she had promised to give it.

She found she loved him with a depth and a passion she had not been aware of. But he had gone away without a goodbye to her, in anger, and with Miss Deane. He would never have done that if there had been a spark of love left in his heart for her.

Where and how was he going to spend that week or ten days? At the house of Miss Deane's parents, sitting beside her, hearing her talk and enjoying it, though he knew his little wife at home must be breaking her heart because of his absence?

Was he doing this instead of carrying out his threat of locking her up? Did he know that this was a punishment ten times worse?

But if he wasn't going to love her any more, if he was tired of her and wanted to be rid of her, how could she ever bear to stay and be a burden and constant annoyance to him?

Elsie, coming up a little later, found her in her boudoir crying bitterly.

"Dear child, my dear little daughter," she said taking her in her kind arms, "don't grieve so. A week or ten days will soon roll round and Edward will be with you again."

"Oh, mamma, it is a long, long while!" she sobbed. "You know we've never been parted for a whole day since we were married and he's all I have."

"Yes, dear, I know. And I felt sure you were crying up here and didn't want to show your telltale face at the table, so I sent your breakfast up. I hope you paid it proper attention—did not treat it with neglect?" she added sportively.

"It tasted very good, mamma, and you were very kind to send it," Zoe said.

She longed to ask where and on what errand Edward had gone, but did not want to expose her ignorance of his plans.

"I did not know the ladies were going home today," she remarked.

"It was very sudden," was the reply. "A telegram received this morning summoned them home because of the alarming illness of Miss Deane's father. And as Edward had business to attend to that would make it necessary for him to take a train leaving only an hour later than theirs, he thought it best to see them on their way as far as our city. He could not do more, as their destination and his lie in exactly opposite directions."

Though Edward had kept his own counsel, the kind mother had her suspicions and was anxious to relieve Zoe's mind as far as lay in her power.

Zoe's brightening countenance and a great sigh of relief showed Elsie that her efforts were not altogether in vain.

"I think Edward was very sorry to leave his little wife so long," she went on. "He committed her to my care. What will you do with yourself this morning, dear, while I am busy with the children in the schoolroom?"

"I don't know, mamma, perhaps learn some lessons. Edward would wish me to attend to my studies while he is away, and I want to please him."

"I haven't a doubt of that, dear. I know there is a very strong love between you, and the knowledge makes me very happy."

"Mamma," said Zoe, "may I ask you a question?"

"Certainly, dear, as many as you please."

"Did you obey your husband?"

Elsie looked surprised, almost startled. The query seemed to throw new light on the state of affairs between Edward and his young wife, but she answered promptly in her own sweet, gentle tones. "My dear, I often wished he would only give me the opportunity. It would have been so great a pleasure to give up my wishes for one I loved so dearly."

"Then he never ordered you?"

"Yes, once—very soon after our marriage—he laid his commands upon me to cease calling him Mr. Travilla and say Edward," Elsie said, with a dreamy smile and a far away look in her soft hazel eyes.

"He was very much older than I. I had known him from very early childhood as a grown up gentleman and my father's friend, and I had been so used to calling him Mr. Travilla, that I could hardly feel it respectful to drop the title.

"The only other order he ever gave me was not to exert myself to lift my little Elsie before I had recovered my strength after her birth. He was very tenderly careful of his 'little wife' as he delighted to call me."

"I wish I had known him," said Zoe. "Please tell me, is my husband much like him?"

"More in looks than disposition. I sometimes think he resembles my father more than his own in the latter regard."

"Yes," thought Zoe, "I'm certain that's where he gets his disposition to domineer over me and order me about. I always knew Grandpa Dinsmore was of that sort."

Aloud she said, with a watery smile, "And my Edward has been very tenderly careful of me."

"And always will be, I trust," said his mother, smiling cheerily. "If he does not prove so, he is less like my father than I think. Mamma will tell you, I am sure, that she has been the happiest of wives."

"I suppose it depends a good deal upon the two dispositions how a couple get on together," remarked Zoe, sagely. "But, mamma, do you think the man should always rule and have his way in everything?"

"I think it a wife's best plan, if she desires to have her own way, is always to be or seem ready to give up to her husband. Don't deny or oppose their claim to authority, and they are not likely to care to exert it."

"If I were only as wise and good as you, mamma!" murmured Zoe with a sigh.

"Ah, dear, I am not at all good. And as to the wisdom, I trust it will come to you with years. There is an old saying that we cannot expect to find grey heads on green shoulders."

Chapter Twenty-First

And if division come, it soon is past,
Too sharp, too strange an agony to last.
And like some river's bright, abundant tide,
Which art or accidental had forc'd aside,
The well-springs of affection gushing o'er,
Back to their natural channels flow once more.

—Mrs. Norton

Left alone, Zoe sat quietly meditating upon her mother-in-law's advice.

"Oh," she said to herself, "if I could only know that my husband's love isn't gone forever, I could take comfort in planning to carry it out. But oh, if he hadn't quite left off caring for me, how could he threaten me so, and then go away without making up, without saying goodbye, even if he didn't kiss me? I couldn't have gone away from him so for one day, and he expects to be away for ten. Ten days! Such a long, long while!" Her tears fell like rain.

She wiped them away after a little, opened her books, and tried to study, but she could not fix her mind upon the subject. Her thoughts would wander from it to Edward, traveling farther and farther from her, and her tears kept dropping on the page.

She gave it up and tried to sew, but could not see to take her stitches or thread her needle for the blinding tears.

So she put on her hat and a veil to hide her tear-stained face and swollen eyes, stole quietly downstairs and out into the grounds, where she wandered about solitary and sad.

Everywhere she missed Edward. She could think of nothing but him and his displeasure, and her heart was filled with sad forebodings for the future. Would he ever, ever love and be kind to her again?

After a while she crept back to her apartments, taking care to avoid meeting anyone.

But Elsie was there looking for her. The children's lesson hours were over. They were going for a drive and hoped Zoe would go along.

"Thank you, mamma, but I do not care to go today," Zoe answered, in a choking voice, and turned away to hide her tears.

"My dear child, my dear, foolish, little girl!" Elsie said, putting her arms around her. "Why should you grieve so? Ned will soon be at home again, if all goes well. He is not very far away, and if you should become ill or need him very much for any reason, a telegram would bring him to you in a few hours' time."

"But he went without kissing me goodbye. He didn't kiss me last night or this morning." The words were on the tip of Zoe's tongue, but she held them back and answered only with fresh tears and sobs.

"I'm afraid you are not well, dear," Elsie said. "What can I do for you?"

"Nothing, thank you, mamma. I didn't sleep quite so well as usual last night, and my head aches. I'll lie down and try to get a nap."

"Do, dear, and I hope it will relieve the poor head. As you are a healthy little body, I presume the pain has been brought on merely by loss of sleep and crying. I think Edward must not leave you for so long a time again. Would you like mamma to stay with you, darling?" she asked, with a motherly caress.

Zoe declined the offer. She would be more likely to sleep if quite alone, and Elsie withdrew after seeing her comfortably established upon the bed.

"Strange," she said to herself as she passed through the upper hall and down the broad staircase into the lower one. "It can hardly be that Edward's absence alone can distress her so greatly. I fear there is some misunderstanding between them. I think I must telegraph for Edward if she continues so inconsolable. His wife's health and happiness are of far more consequence than any business matter. But I should consult papa first, of course."

She went into the library, found him sitting there, and laid the case before him.

He shared her fear that all was not right between the young couple, and remarked that, unfortunately, Edward had too much of his grandfather's sternness and disposition to domineer.

"I don't like to hear you depreciate yourself, papa," Elsie said. "Edward may have that disposition without having got it from you. And I am sure mamma would indignantly repel the insinuation that you were a domineering husband."

"Perhaps so, my daughter was the safety valve in my case. Well, daughter, my advice is wait till tomorrow at all events. I must say she doesn't seem to me one of the kind to submit tamely to oppression. I did not like her behavior last evening, and it may be that she needs the lesson her husband seems to be giving her. He certainly has been affectionate enough in the past to make it reasonable to suppose he is not abusing her now."

"Oh, I could never think he would do that!" exclaimed his mother. "I believe in my heart he would hurry home at once if he knew how she is fretting over his absence."

It was near the dinner hour when Elsie returned from her drive. Stealing on tiptoe into Zoe's bedroom, she found her fast asleep. Her eyelashes were still wet, and she looked flushed and feverish.

Elsie gazed at her in tender pity and some little anxiety. The face was so young and childlike and even in sleep wore a grieved expression that touched the kind, mother heart.

"Poor little orphan!" she sighed to herself. "She must feel very lonely and forlorn in her husband's absence, especially if things have gone wrong between them. How could I ever have borne a word or look of displeasure from my husband? I hope she is not going to be ill."

"Is Zoe not coming down?" Mr. Dinsmore asked as the family gathered about the dinner table.

"I found her sleeping, papa, and thought it best not to wake her," Elsie answered. "I think she does not look quite well, and that sleep will do her more good than anything else."

Zoe slept most of the afternoon, woke apparently more cheerful, and ate with seeming enjoyment the delicate lunch presently brought by Elsie's orders. But she steadily declined to join the family at tea or in the parlor.

She would much rather stay where she was for the rest of the day, she said, as she felt dull and her head still ached a little.

Everyone felt concerned about and disposed to be as kind to her as possible. Mrs. Dinsmore, Elsie, Violet, and Rosie all came in in the course of the afternoon and evening. They asked how she fared, expressed the hope that she would soon be quite well again, and tried to cheer her up.

They offered her companionship through the night. Any one of them would willingly sleep with her, but she said she was not timid and would actually prefer to remain alone.

"Well, dear, I should feel a trifle easier not to have you alone," Elsie said as she bade her good night. "But we will not force our company upon you. None of us lock our doors at night, and my rooms are not far away. Do not hesitate to wake me if you feel uneasy or want anything in the night."

"Thank you, dear mamma," returned Zoe, putting her arms about her mother's neck. "You are so good and kind! Such a dear mother to me! I will do as you say. If I feel at all timid in the night I shall run to your rooms and creep into bed with you."

So they left her, and the house grew silent and still in its usual way.

It was the first night since her marriage that her husband had not been with her, and she missed him more than ever. Through the day she had been buoyed up by the hope that he would send her a note, a telegram, or some sort of message.

He had not done so, and the conviction that she had quite alienated him grew stronger and stronger.

She again indulged in bitter weeping, wetting her pillow with her tears as she vainly courted sleep.

"He hates me now; I know he does, and he will never love me again," she repeated to herself. "I wish I didn't love him so. He said he was sorry he couldn't give me my liberty, but I don't want it. But he wants to be rid of me, or he would never have said that. And how unhappy he must be, and will be for the rest of his life, tied to a wife he hates.

"I won't stay here to be a burden and a torment to him!" she cried, starting up with sudden determination and energy. "I love him so dearly that I'll deliver him from that, even though it will break my heart. Oh, how can I live without him?"

She considered a moment, and the foolish child actually thought it would be an act of noble self-sacrifice. She somehow thought it also very romantic, to run away and die of a broken heart, in order to relieve her husband of the burden and torment she chose to imagine that he considered her.

A folly that was partly the effect of too much reading of sensational novels, partly of a physical ailment, for she was really feverish and ill.

She did not pause to decide where she would go, or to reflect how she could support herself. Were not all places alike away from the one she so dearly loved? And as to support, she had a little money and would not be likely to live long enough to need more.

Perhaps Edward would search for her from a sense of duty—she knew he was very conscientious—but she would manage so that he would never be able to find her. She would go under an assumed name. She would call herself Miss, and no one would suspect her of being a married woman running away from her husband. Ah, it was not altogether a disadvantage to be and look so young!

And when she should find herself dying or so near it there would not be time to send for Edward, she would tell someone who she really was and ask that a letter should be written to him telling of her death. This way he would know he was free to marry again.

Marry again! The thought of that possibility shook her resolution for a moment. It was torture to imagine the love and caresses that had been hers lavished upon another woman.

But, perhaps, after his unhappy experience of married life, he would choose to live single the rest of his days. He had his mother and sisters to love, and he probably could be happy without a wife.

Besides, she had read somewhere that though love was everything to a woman, men were of a different sort and do quite well without it.

She went into the dressing room, turned up the night lamp, and looked at her watch.

It was one o'clock. At two o'clock a stage passed northward along a road on the farther side of Fairview. She could easily make her few preparations in half an hour, walk to the nearest point on the route of the stage in time to stop it and get in, then while journeying on, decide what her next step should be.

She packed a handbag with such things as she deemed essential. She arrayed herself in a plain, dark, woolen dress with hat, veil, and gloves to match, threw a shawl over her arm, and was just turning to go when a thought struck her.

"I ought to leave a note to him, of course. They always do."

Sitting down at her writing desk, she directed an envelope to her husband, then wrote on a card:

I am going away never to come back.
Don't look for me, for it will be quite useless,
as I shall manage so that you can never trace me. It breaks my heart to leave
you, my dear, dear husband, for I love you better than life.
But I know I have lost your love, and
I want to rid you of the burden and annoyance of a hated wife. So, farewell
forever in this world, and may you be very happy all your days.
Zoe

Her tears fell fast as she wrote. She had to wipe them away again and again, and the card was so blotted and blistered by them that some of the words were scarcely legible, but there was not time to write another. So, she put it in the envelope and laid it on the dressing table where it would be sure to catch his eye.

Then, taking up her shawl and satchel, she sent one tearful farewell glance around the room and stole noiselessly downstairs and out of the house by a side door. It caught her dress in closing, but she was unaware of that for a moment. As she stood still on the step, remembering with a sudden pang that was more than half regret that the deed was done beyond recall for the dead-latch was down and she had no key with which to effect an entrance. She must go on now, whether she would or not.

She took a step forward and found she was fast. She could neither go nor retreat. Oh, dreadful to be caught there and her scheme at the same time baffled and revealed!

All at once she saw it in a new light. Oh, how angry, how very angry Edward would be! What would he do and say to her? Certainly, she had given him sufficient reason to deem it necessary to lock her up. For what right had she to go away to stay without his knowledge and consent? She who had taken a solemn vow—in the presence of her dying father, too—to love, honor and obey him as long as they both should live. Oh, it would be too disgraceful to be caught so!

She exerted all her strength in the effort to wrench herself free, even at the cost of tearing the dress—being obliged to travel with it unrepaired. But, in vain, the material was too strong to give way, and she sank down on the step in a state of pitiable fright and despair.

She heard the clock in the hall strike two. Even the servants would not be stirring before five, so she had at least three hours to sit there alone and exposed to danger from tramps, thieves, and burglars, if any should happen to come about.

And oh, the miserable prospect before her when this trying vigil should be over. How grieved mamma would be—dear mamma, whom she loved with true daughterly affection. How stern and angry Grandpa Dinsmore, how astonished and displeased all the others, how wicked and supremely silly they would think her!

Perhaps she could bribe the servants to keep her secret—her dress, her traveling bag, and the early hour would reveal something of its nature. If only she could gain her rooms again without being seen by any of the family. But then her life would be one of constant terror of discovery.

Should she try that course, or the more truthful one of not attempting any concealment?

She was still debating this question in her mind when her heart almost flew into her mouth at the sound of a man's step approaching on the gravel walk. It drew nearer, nearer, came close to her side, and with a cry of terror, she fell in a little heap on the doorstep in a dead faint.

He uttered a low exclamation of astonishment, stooped over her, and pushed aside her veil so that the moonlight shone full upon her face. "Zoe!" he cried. "Is it possible? What could have brought you here at this hour of the night?"

He paused for an answer, but none came. Then, bending lower and perceiving that she was quite unconscious and also held fast by the door, he took a key from his pocket and opened the door.

"Running away, evidently! Could anyone have conceived the possibility of her doing so crazy a thing!" he muttered, as he took her in his arms.

Then a dark thought crossed his mind, but he put it determinedly from him.

"No, I will not, cannot think it! She is pure, guileless, and innocent as an infant."

He stooped again, picked up the bag, closed the door softly, and carried her upstairs—treading with caution lest a stumble or the sound of his footsteps should arouse someone and lead to the discovery of what was going on. Yet, he went with as great celerity as consistent with that caution, fearing consciousness might return too soon for the preservation of the secrecy he desired.

But it did not, and she was still insensible when he laid her down on a couch in her boudoir.

He took off her hat and veil, threw them aside, loosened her dress, opened a window to give her air, then went into the dressing room for the night lamp usually kept burning there.

As he turned it up, his eye fell upon Zoe's note.

He knew her handwriting instantly.

"Here is the explanation," was the thought that flashed into his mind, and he snatched it up and tore open the envelope. He then held the card near the light to read what her fingers had traced scarcely an hour ago.

His eyes filled as he read, and two great drops fell as he laid it down.

He picked up the lamp and hastened back to her.

As he drew near she opened her eyes, sent one frightened glance round the room and up into his pale, troubled face, then covering hers with her hands, burst into hysterical weeping.

He set down the lamp, knelt by her sofa, and gathered her in his arms—resting her head against his shoulder.

"Zoe, my little Zoe, my own dear wife!" he said in faltering accents. "Have I really been so cruel that you despair of my love? Why, my darling, no greater calamity than your loss could possibly befall me! I love you dearly, dearly! Better far than I did when I asked you to be mine—when we gave ourselves to each other."

"Oh, is it true? Do you really love me yet in spite of all my jealousy and willfulness, and—and—oh, I have been very bad and ungrateful and so very troublesome!" she sobbed, clinging about his neck.

"And I have been too dictatorial and stern," he said, kissing her again and again. "I have not had the patience I ought to have had with my little girl-wife. I have not been very forbearing and as kind as I meant to be."

"Indeed, Edward, you have been very patient and forbearing," she returned. "And you would never have been cross to me if I hadn't provoked you beyond endurance. I have been very bad to you, dear Ned, but if you'll keep me and love me I'll try to behave better."

"I'll do both," he said holding her closer and repeating his caresses.

"Oh, I'm so glad, so glad!" she cried, with the tears running over her cheeks. "So glad I have to weep for joy. I've been breaking my heart since you went away and left me in anger and without one word of goodbye."

"My poor darling, it was too cruel," he sighed. "I found I could not stand it any more than you and had to come back to make it up to you. Oh, but I frightened you quite terribly down there at the door, did I not?"

"Oh, Ned," she murmured, hiding her blushing face on his chest. "How very good you are to be so loving and kind when you have a right to be angry and stern with me. You haven't even asked what I was doing down there in the night."

"Your note explained that," he said in moved tones, thinking how great must have been the distress that led to such an act. "For I fear I am just as much deserving of reproof as yourself."

"Then you forgive me?" she asked humbly. "I thought I had a right to go away, thinking it would make you happier, but now I know I had no right, because I had promised myself to you for all my life."

"No, neither of us has a right to forsake the other—we 'are no more twain but one flesh. What, therefore, God has joined together, let no man put asunder.' We are husband and wife for as long as we both shall live, and must dwell together in mutual love and forbearance. We will exchange forgiveness, dearest, for we have both been to blame, and I forgive your attempt tonight on the sole condition that you promise me never, never to do such a thing again."

"I promise." She continued imploringly, "Oh, Ned, won't you keep my secret? I couldn't bear to have it known even in the family."

"No more could I, love," he answered. "Oh, but I am thankful that you were caught by the door and so prevented from carrying out your purpose!"

"So am I, and that it was my own dear husband and not a burglar, as I feared, who found me there."

"Ah, was that the cause of your fright?" he asked, with a look of relief and pleasure. "I thought it was your terror of your husband's wrath that caused your faint. But, darling, you are looking weary and actually ill. You must go to bed at once."

"I'll obey you, this time and always," she answered, looking up fondly into his face. "I am convinced now that I am only a foolish child in need of guidance and control. Who should provide them but you? I could hardly stand it from anybody else—unless mamma—but I'm sure that in the future it will be a pleasure to take it from my own dear husband if—if only—" she paused, blushing and hiding her face again.

"If what, my love?"

"If only instead of 'You must and shall,' you will say kindly, 'I want you to do it to please me, Zoe.'"

"Sweet one," he answered, holding her to his heart, "I do fully intend that it shall be always love and coaxing after this."

Chapter Twenty-Second

Our love, it ne'er was reckoned,
Yet good it is and true;
It's half the world to me, dear,
It's all the world to you.

—Hood

Edward was a trifle late in obeying the call to breakfast. He found the rest of the family already seated at the table, and great was the surprise created by his grand entrance.

"Why, how's this? Hae we all been sleepin' a week or ten days?" exclaimed Mr. Lilburn. "The lad was to hae been absent that length o' time, and I though it was but yesterday he went. Yet, here he is in the flesh!"

"This is an unexpected pleasure, my dear boy," was his mother's greeting.

The others said "Good morning," and all smilingly awaited an explanation.

"Good morning to you all," returned Edward, taking his seat. "Of course, I have not had time to attend to the business matter that took me away. But, the fact is, I found I could not do without my wife, so came back after her."

"Where is she now?" asked his mother.

"I left her still in bed and asleep. I came home by the stage, found her awake—indeed, I think she said she had not slept at all—and kept her awake for some time talking."

"So much to say after so lengthened a separation?" laughingly interrupted his grandfather.

"Yes, sir, a good deal," Edward answered, coloring slightly. "So she has to make it up now, and I would not wake her."

"Quite right," said his mother. "Her breakfast shall be sent up whenever she is ready for it."

"I'm very glad you've come, Ned," remarked Rosie. "For Zoe nearly cried her eyes out yesterday, grieving for you. 'Twouldn't be I that would fret so after any man living—unless it might be grandpa," she quipped with a coquettish, laughing look at him.

"Thank you, my dear," he said.

"Ah, lassie, that's a' because your time hasna come yet," remarked Mr. Lilburn. "When it does, you'll be as lovelorn and foolish as the rest."

"Granting that it is foolish for a woman to love her husband," put in Mrs. Dinsmore sportively.

"A heresy never to be countenanced here," said her spouse. "Both the husbands and wives of this family expect to give and receive no small amount of that commodity. Then, do you set off again this morning, Ned?"

"No, sir, not before tomorrow—not then unless Zoe is ready to go with me."

"Quite right, my boy. Your wife's health and her happiness are, as your mother remarked to me yesterday, of far more consequence than any mere business matter."

On leaving the table, Edward followed his mother out to the veranda.

"Can I have a word in private with you, mamma?" he asked, and she thought his look was quite troubled.

"Certainly," she said. "I hope nothing is wrong with our little Zoe?"

"It is of her—and myself I want to speak. I feel compelled to make a confession to you, mother dear, that I would not willingly do so to anyone else. Perhaps you have suspected," he added, coloring with mortification, "that all was not right between us when I left yesterday. She would not have fretted so over my mere absence of a few days, but I had scolded and threatened her the night before and went away without any reconciliation or even a goodbye. In fact, she was asleep when I left the rooms and knew nothing of my going."

"Oh, Edward!" exclaimed his listener in a low, pained tone.

"I am bitterly ashamed of my conduct, mother," he said with emotion. "But we have made it up and are both very happy again in each other's love. She was very humble over her part of the quarrel, poor little thing! We mean to live in peace and love the rest of our days, God helping us," he added reverently.

"I trust so, my dear boy," Elsie said. "For whether you live in peace or contention will make all the difference of happiness or misery in your lives. It would have quite broken my heart had your father ever scolded or threatened me."

"But you, mamma, were a woman when you married—old enough and wise enough to guide and control yourself."

"I was older than Zoe is, that is true. But you've no right to be dictatorial, Edward. If you must rule, do it by love and persuasion. You will find it the easiest and happiest way for both of you."

"Yes, mother, I am convinced of that now. But unfortunately for my poor little wife, I have not my father's gentleness and easy temper. Will you come up with me now and take a look at her? I fear she is not quite well—her cheeks are so flushed and her hands so hot. I shall never forgive myself if I have made her ill."

"I sincerely hope you are not to be visited with so severe a punishment as that," his mother said. "But come, let us go to her at once."

They found her still sleeping, but not profoundly. Her face was unnaturally flushed and wore a very troubled expression, while her breathing seemed quite labored.

As they stood anxiously regarding her, she awoke with a sharp cry of distress and anguish. As she caught sight of her husband bending over her, her face grew radiant, and she threw her arms about his neck. "Oh, Ned, dear Ned!" she cried. "Are you here? And do you love me yet?"

"Dearly, dearly, my darling," he said, holding her close. "What has troubled you?"

"Oh, such a dreadful dream! I thought I was all alone in a desert and couldn't find you anywhere."

"But 'drames always go by contraries, my dear,'" he quoted sportively. Then more seriously, "Are you quite well, love?" he asked.

"A little dull and a trifle headachy," she answered, smiling up at him. "But I think a cup of coffee and a drive with my husband in the sweet, morning air will cure me."

"You shall have both with the least possible delay."

"What time is it? Have you been to breakfast?"

"It's about nine, and I have taken breakfast. I think you must have some before exerting yourself to dress."

"Just as you say. It's nice to have you tell me what to do," she said, nestling closer in his arms. "I can't think why I should ever have disliked it."

"I presume it was all the fault in my tone and manner—sometimes of my words, too," he said, passing his hand caressingly over her hair and cheek. "I'm afraid I've been decidedly bearish on several occasions. But I trust I shall have the grace to treat my wife with politeness and consideration after this."

Elsie, who had left the room on Zoe's awakening, now came in and bade her an affectionate good morning. She told them she had ordered Zoe's breakfast to be brought up at once, adding, "I hope you will do it justice, my dear."

"I'll see that she does, mamma," Edward answered for her, in sportive tone. "She has made such fair promises of submission, obedience, and all that, that she'll hardly dare refuse to do anything I bid her."

"I haven't been very good about it lately, mamma," Zoe said looking tearfully, but smilingly from one to the other. "But Ned's forgiven me, and now I feel as you say you did—that it's a real pleasure to give up my wishes to one I love so very deeply, and who is, I know, much wiser than I."

"That is right, my dear," Elsie said tenderly. "And I trust he will show himself worthy of all your love and confidence."

The two now comported themselves like a pair of lovers—as indeed they had done through all their brief married life, except the last few days.

Edward exerted himself for the entertainment of his little wife during their drive and was really very tender and careful of her.

On their return, he bade her lie down on the sofa in her boudoir and rest, saying that she looked languid and unlike herself.

"To please you," she said, obeying the mandate with a smiling glance up into his face.

"That's a good wife!" he responded, sitting down beside her and smoothing her hair with a fond, caressing hand. "Now, what shall I do to please you, my darling?"

"Stay here, close beside me, hold my hand, and talk to me."

"Very well," he answered, closing his fingers over the hand she put into his, then lifting it to his lips. "How your face has changed, love, since that frightened look it held when I came in with the lamp last night."

"How frightened and ashamed I was, Ned!" she exclaimed, tears springing to her eyes. "I felt that you had a right to beat me if you wanted to, and I shouldn't have said a word if you'd done it."

"But you couldn't have feared that?" he said, with a pained look and coloring deeply.

"No, oh, no, indeed! I know you would never do that, but I dreaded what you might say. I did not at all expect you would be so kind and forgiving and loving to me.

"But how was I brought up here? I knew nothing from the instant you were at my side on the door-step till I saw you coming in with the lamp."

"In your husband's arms."

"What a heavy load for you to carry!" she said, looking at him with concern.

"No, not at all. I did it with perfect ease, except for the darkness and the fear that you might recover consciousness on the way and scream out with fright before you discovered who your captor was."

"My husband, my dear husband!" she murmured, softly stroking his face as he bent over her to press a kiss upon her forehead.

"My darling little wife," he returned.

Then, after a moment's silent exchange of caresses, he asked with a slight smile, "Would you mind telling me where you were going and what you intended to do when you got there?"

"I have no right to refuse you, if you require a full and complete confession," she said playfully and blushed deeply.

"I don't require it, but should like to have it from you, nevertheless. I confess my curiosity is piqued," he said with an amused, yet tender look and tone.

"There isn't really very much to tell," she sighed. "Only that I was dreadfully unhappy and had worked myself up to believing that I was a hated wife and a burden and annoyance to my husband, I thought it would be an act of noble self-sacrifice to run away and— oh, Ned, please don't laugh at me!"

"I am not laughing, love," he said in soothing, tremulous tones, taking her in his arms and holding her close as he had done the night before. "How could I laugh at you for being willing to sacrifice everything for me? But that's not all?"

"Not quite. It came to me like a flash that the stage passed so near at two o'clock in the morning, and that I could get away then without being seen, and after I was in it make up my mind where I would get out."

"And how did you expect to support yourself?"

"There was some money in my purse—you never let it get empty, Ned—and—and—I thought I wouldn't need any very long."

"Wouldn't? Why not?"

"Oh, I was sure, so sure I couldn't live for very long without you," she cried, hugging him close and ending with a burst of tears and sobs.

"You dear, dear little thing!" he said with great emotion, tightening his clasp of her slight form. "After I had been so cruel to you, too!"

"No, you weren't, except in going away without making up and saying goodbye."

"It's very generous of you to say it, darling. But how large was this sum of money that you expected to last as long as you needed any?"

"I don't know. I didn't stop to count it. You can do that, if you want to. I suppose the purse is still in my satchel."

He brought the satchel, still unpacked, took out the purse, and examined its contents.

"Barely ten dollars," he said. "It would have lasted but a few days, and, my darling, what would have become of you then?"

He bent over her in grave tenderness.

"I don't know, Ned," she replied. "I suppose I'd have had to look for employment."

"To think of you, my delicate, coddled darling, looking for employment by which to earn her daily bread!" he exclaimed with emotion. "It is plain you know nothing of the hardships and difficulties you would have had to encounter. I shudder to think of it all. But I should never have let it come to that."

"Would you have looked for me, Ned?"

"I should have begun the search the instant I heard of your flight, nor ever have known a moment's rest till I found you!" he exclaimed with energy. "But as I came in the stage you proposed to take, I should have met and brought you back, if that fortunate mishap had not taken place."

Then she told him of her thoughts, feelings, and painful anticipations while held fast in the relentless grasp of the door, finishing with, "Oh, I never could have dreamed that it would all end so well, so happily for me!"

"And yet, dear one, I do not think you at all realize how painful— not to say dreadful—would have been the consequences to you, to me, and, indeed to all the family, if you had succeeded in carrying out what I must call your crazy scheme."

She looked up at him in alarmed inquiry. He went on, "'Madame Rumor, with her thousand tongues,' would have had many a tale to tell of the cruel abuse to which you had been subjected by your husband and his family—so cruel you were compelled to run away in the night, taking advantage of the temporary absence of your tyrannical husband while—"

"Oh, Ned, dear Ned, I never thought of that!" she exclaimed, interrupting him with a burst of tears and sobs. "I wouldn't for the world have wrought harm to you or any of them."

"No, love, I know you wouldn't. I believe your motives were altogether kind and self-sacrificing," he said soothingly. "And you yourself would have been the greatest sufferer. The world judges very hardly—how hardly my little girl-wife has no idea. Wicked people would have found wicked motives to which to impute your act and caused a stain upon your fair fame that might never have been removed for all your days.

"But there, there, love, do not cry any more over it. Happily, the whole thing is a secret between us two, and we may now dismiss the disagreeable subject forever.

"But shall we not promise each other that we will never part in anger, even when the separation may not be for an hour? Or even lie down to sleep at night unreconciled, if there has been the slightest misunderstanding or coldness between us?"

"Oh, yes, yes, I promise!" she cried eagerly. "But oh, dear Ned, I hope we will never, never have any more coldness or quarreling between us, never say a cross word to each other ever again."

"And I join you, dearest, in both the wish and the promise."

"I am growing very babyish," she said presently with a wistful look up into his face. "I can hardly bear to think of being parted from you for a day, and I suppose you still must attend to that business affair?"

"Yes, as soon as I see that my wife is quite well enough to undertake the journey—for I'm not going again without her."

"Oh, will you take me with you, Ned?" she cried joyfully. "How very good of you."

"Good to myself, little woman," he said, smiling down at her. "It will turn a tiresome business trip into a pleasure excursion. I have always found my enjoyment doubled by the companionship of my better half."

"I call that rank heresy," she said laughing. "You're the better half as well as the bigger. I wish I were worthy of such a good husband," she added earnestly and with a look of loving admiration. "I'm very proud of you, my dear—so good and wise and handsome as you are!"

"Oh, hush, hush! Such fulsome flattery," he returned, coloring and laughing. "Let me see. This is Friday, so near the end of the week that I do not care to leave home till next week. We will say Tuesday morning next, if that will suit you, love?"

"Quite nicely," she answered. "Oh, I'm so glad you have promised to take me with you!"

Chapter Twenty-Third

Lulu

$\mathscr{B}$efore two days had passed, Zoe was quite herself again. She was as full of delight at the prospect of going away for a little trip as any child could have been. She wore so bright a face, was so merry and frolicsome, that it was a pleasure to watch her—especially when with her husband and not aware that any other eye was upon her.

His face, too, beamed with happiness.

Elsie's eyes resting upon them would sometimes fill with tears—half of joy in their felicity, half of sorrowful yet tender reminiscence. In his present mood, Edward was very like his father in looks, in speech, in manner.

Tuesday morning came at last, bringing with it delightful weather. Edward had decided to take a later train than when starting before, because he would not have Zoe roused too soon from sleep.

They took breakfast with the family at the usual hour, an open barouche waiting for them at the door. Then, with a happy good-bye to all, set out upon their journey, driving to the nearest station and there taking the train.

"I wish I was going, too!" sighed Lulu as she and Rosie stood looking after the barouche.

"Mamma would have let us drive over to the station with them," said Rosie. "Edward asked if we might, but Ben had some errands to do in town, and couldn't bring us back in time for lessons."

"Lessons! I'm sick and tired of them!" grumbled Lulu. "Other children had holidays last week, but we had to go right on studying."

"But we are to take ours in a week or two, visiting at the Oaks and the Laurels—perhaps two weeks at each place. I'm sure that will be far nicer than to have had Easter holidays at home."

"There, it's out of sight," said Lulu. "I'd like to be Aunt Zoe, just starting off on a journey. Let's take a run down the avenue, Rosie."

"I would, but I must look over my Latin lesson, or I may not be ready for grandpa."

With the last words she turned and went away into the house.

Lulu knew that she was not ready for Mr. Dinsmore either, but she was in no mood for study. The grounds looked so inviting that she yielded to the temptation to take a ramble instead.

From his window, Max saw her wandering about among the shrubs and flowers and longed to join her. He was bearing his punishment in a very good spirit—making no complaint, spending his time in study, reading, writing, and carving.

Mr. Dinsmore came to him to hear his recitations and was always able to commend them as excellent. He treated the boy in a kind, fatherly manner— talking to him of his sin and the way to obtain forgiveness and deliverance from it, very much as Elsie and Violet had.

Yet he did not harp continually upon that, but he dwelt often upon other themes, trying so to treat the lad that his self-respect might be restored.

Max appreciated the kindness shown him and was strengthened in his good resolutions. He was privately much troubled about his losses. He was particularly disturbed over the watch, supposing it to be in Ralph's possession—for Mr. Dinsmore had said nothing to him on the subject.

Being very fond of his sisters, Max keenly felt the separation from them no small part of his punishment. He followed Lulu's movements this morning with wistful eyes.

She looked up and saw his rather pale, sad face at the window. So she drew nearer and called softly to him, "Max, how are you? I'm so sorry for you."

He only shook his head and turned away.

Then Mr. Dinsmore's voice spoke sternly from a lower window, "Lulu you are disobeying orders. Go into the house and to the schoolroom immediately. You ought to have been there fully a quarter of an hour ago."

Lulu was a little frightened and obeyed at once.

"You are late, Lulu. You must try to be more punctual in the future," Elsie said in a tone of mild rebuke, as the little girl sat down at her desk.

"I don't care if I am," she muttered insolently.

Rosie darted at her a look of angry astonishment, Gracie looked shocked, and little Walter said, "It's very, very naughty to speak so to my mamma."

But Elsie did not seem to have heard; her face still wore its usual sweet, placid expression. Lulu thought she had not heard but found out her mistake when she went forward to recite. She was told in a gentle, quiet tone, "You are not my pupil, today, Lulu." She returned to her seat overwhelmed with embarrassment and anger.

No further notice was taken of her by anyone except Gracie, who now and then stole a troubled, pitying look at her, until Mr. Dinsmore came to hear the Latin lessons.

Lulu had sat idly at her desk nursing her anger and discontent—her eyes on the book open before her, but her thoughts elsewhere. Therefore, she was not prepared for him.

Lulu was frightened, but tried to hide it. She made an attempt to answer the first question put to her, but broke down in confusion.

He asked another. She was unable to answer it, and with a frown he said, "I perceive that you know nothing about your lesson today. Why have you not learned it?"

"Because I didn't feel like it," quietly muttered the little delinquent.

Rosie opened her eyes wide in astonishment. She would never have dared to answer her grandfather in that manner.

"Take your book and learn it now," he said in his sternest tone.

Lulu did not venture to disobey. She was really quite afraid of Mr. Dinsmore.

He heard Rosie's lesson, assigned her task for the next day, and both left the room. The others had gone about the time Mr. Dinsmore came in, so Lulu was left alone.

She thought it best to give her mind to the lesson, and in half an hour, felt that she was fully prepared with it.

But Mr. Dinsmore did not come back, and she dared not leave the room, though impatient to do so.

The dinner bell rang and still he had not come.

Lulu was hungry and began to fear that she was to be made to fast. But, at length a servant brought her a good, substantial, though plain dinner, set it before her, and silently withdrew.

"It's not half as good as they've got," Lulu remarked aloud to herself, discontentedly eyeing her fare. "But it's better than nothing."

With that philosophical reflection, she fell to work and speedily emptied the dishes.

Mr. Dinsmore came to her shortly after, heard her lesson, gave her a little serious talk, and promptly dismissed her.

Feeling that she owed an apology to Grandma Elsie, but still too stubborn and proud to make it, Lulu was ashamed to join the others, so went off alone into the grounds. She was not Grandma Elsie's pupil, she understood, until the morning's impertinence had been atoned for.

It was against the rules to go beyond the boundary of the grounds without permission. Yet, after wandering through them for a while, she did so. She entered a shady, pleasant road and walked on without any settled purpose. At length, she reached a neighboring plantation where lived some little girls with whom she had a slight acquaintance.

They were playing croquet on the lawn, and espying Lulu at the gate, invited her to come in and join them.

She did so, became much interested in the sport, and forgot to go home until the lengthening shadows warned her that it must be very near the tea hour at Ion.

She then bid a hasty goodbye and retraced her steps with great expedition and in no tranquil state of mind. In truth, she was a good deal alarmed as she thought of the possible consequences to herself of her bold disregard of the rules.

She arrived at Ion heated and out of breath, and, as a glance at the hall clock told her, fully fifteen minutes late.

Hair and dress were in some disorder, but not thinking of that in her haste and perturbation, she went directly to the supper room, where the family were in the midst of their meal.

They all seemed busily engaged with it or in some form of conversation, and she hoped to slip unobserved into her seat.

But to her consternation she perceived, as she drew near, that neither plate nor chair seemed to have been set for her—every place was occupied.

At the same instant, Mr. Dinsmore, turning a stern look upon her remarked, "We have no place here for the rebellious and insubordinate. Therefore, I have ordered your plate removed. And while you continue to belong to that class, you will take your meals in your own room."

He dismissed her with a wave of his hand as he spoke. Filled with anger and chagrin, she turned and flew from the room, never stopping till she gained her own and slammed the door behind her.

"Before Mr. Lilburn and everybody—the entire family!" she exclaimed aloud, stamping her foot in impotent rage.

Then, catching sight of her figure in the glass, she stood still and gazed, her cheeks reddening more and more with mortification. Hair and dress were tumbled, the latter slightly soiled with the dust of the road. Her boots were also, and the frill about her neck was crushed and partly tucked in.

She set to work with energy to make herself neat, and had scarcely completed the task when her supper was brought in. It consisted of an abundance of rich, sweet milk, fruit, and the nicest of bread and butter.

She ate heartily. Then as Agnes carried away the tray, seated herself by the window with her elbows on the sill, her chin in her hands, and involuntarily took a mental review of the day.

The retrospect was not agreeable.

"And I'll have to tell papa all about it in my diary," she groaned to herself. "No, I sha'n't! What's the use? It'll just make him feel badly. But he said I must, and he trusted me. He trusted me to tell the truth and the whole truth, and I can't deceive him. I can't hide anything from him."

With a heavy sigh she took her writing desk, set it on the sill to catch the fading light, and wrote:

"It has been a bad day for me. I didn't look over my lessons before school, as I ought to have done, but went out in the grounds instead. While I was there, I broke a rule. Grandpa Dinsmore reproved me and called me in. I went up to the schoolroom. Grandma Elsie said I was late and must be more punctual, and I gave her a saucy answer. She wouldn't hear my lessons, and I was cross and wouldn't study. So, I wasn't ready for Grandpa Dinsmore and was saucy to him, too. So I had to stay up there in the schoolroom and learn my lesson over and eat my dinner there by myself.

"After that, when he let me out, I took a long walk and played croquet with some other girls—all without leave.

"They were eating supper when I got back, and I went in without making myself neat. My plate and chair had been taken away, and I was sent up here to take my supper and stay till I'm ready to behave better."

She read over what she had written.

"Oh, what a bad report! How sad it will make papa feel when he reads it!" she thought, tears springing to her eyes.

She pushed the desk aside and leaned on the sill again, her face hidden in her hands. Her father's words about the kindness and generosity of Mr. Dinsmore and his daughter in offering to share their home with his children came to her recollection. All the favors received at the hands of these kindest of friends passed in review before her. Could her own mother have been kinder than Grandma Elsie? And she had repaid her this day with ingratitude, disobedience, and impertinence. How despicably mean!

Tears of shame and penitence began to fall from her eyes, and soon she was sobbing aloud.

Violet heard her cries and came to her side.

"What is it, Lulu, dear? Are you sorry for your misconduct?" she asked in gentle, affectionate tones, smoothing the child's hair with her soft, white hand as she spoke.

"Yes, Mamma, Vi," sobbed the little girl. "Won't you please tell Grandma Elsie I'm sorry I was saucy and disobedient to her this morning?"

"Yes, dear, I will. And—have you not a message for grandpa also?"

"Yes, I'm sorry I was naughty and impertinent to him and for breaking his rules, too. Do you think they'll forgive me, Mamma Vi, and try me again?"

"I am sure they will," Violet said. "And will you not ask God's forgiveness, also, dear child?"

"I do mean to," Lulu said. "And I've told papa all about it. I wish he didn't have to know, because it will make him very sorry."

"Yes," sighed Violet. "It grieves him very much when his dear children do wrong. I hope, dear Lulu, that thought will help you to be good in the future. Still more, that you will learn to hate and forsake sin because it is dishonoring and displeasing to God. It grieves the dear Savior who loves you and died to redeem you."

Forgiveness was readily accorded by both Mr. Dinsmore and his daughter, and Lulu went to bed comparatively happy after a short visit and kind motherly talk from Grandma Elsie.

Two days following Max was released from his imprisonment. He dreaded more than a little to make his appearance downstairs, thinking everyone would view him askance, but was agreeably surprised by being greeted on every hand with the utmost of kindness and cordiality.

On the following Monday Max and the four other children were sent to the Oaks to make their promised visit.

Gracie alone needed some persuasion to induce her to go of her own free will, and that only because mamma was not going. Gracie was not at all sure that she could live two whole weeks without her dear mamma.

Just before they started, Mr. Dinsmore made Max very happy by the restoration of his money and watch. He added an admonition against gambling, and Max replied with an earnest promise never to touch a card again

Chapter Twenty-Fourth

A Chapter of Surprises

Edward and Zoe decided upon a little pleasure trip in addition to the business one, and, in consequence, were absent from home for over a fortnight. On their return, Elsie met them on the threshold with the warmest and most loving of motherly welcomes.

"How well and happy you both look, my dear children!" she said, glancing from one to the other, her face full of proud and fond affection.

"As we are, mother dear," Edward responded. "Glad to see you so, also. How is Vi?"

"Doing nicely."

"Vi! Is she sick?" asked Zoe, her tone expressing both surprise and concern.

"Yes," Elsie said, leading the way down the hall and up the stairs. Then, as they reached the upper hall, she said, "Come this way, my dears, I have something to show you."

She led them to the nursery to the side of a dainty crib. And, pushing aside its curtains of lace, brought to view a little, downy head and a pink face nestling cozily upon the soft pillow within.

Zoe uttered an exclamation of astonishment and delight. "Why, mamma, where did you get it? Oh, the lovely darling!" And down she went on her knees by the side of the crib, to make a closer inspection. "Oh, Ned, just look! Did you ever see anything half so dear and sweet?"

"Yes," he said, with a meaning, laughing look into her sparkling face. "I see something at this moment that to my eyes is dearer and sweeter still. What does Vi think of it all, mamma?" turning to his mother.

"She is very proud and happy," Elsie answered with a smile. "I believe Zoe has echoed Violet's views exactly."

"It's Vi's, is it?" said Zoe. "Come, Ned, do look at it. You ought to care a little about your—"

She broke off with an inquiring glance up into her mother's face.

"Niece," supplied Elsie. "My granddaughter."

"Another Elsie, I suppose," Edward remarked, bending down to examine the little creature with an air of increasing interest.

"Her father must be heard from before the name can be decided upon," his mother answered. "Vi wishes her named for me, but I should prefer to have another Violet."

"I am inclined to think Captain Raymond will agree with her," said Edward.

"I never saw so young a baby," remarked Zoe. "How old is she, mamma?"

"A week, today."

"I'm tempted to break the tenth commandment," said Zoe, leaning over the babe and touching her lips to its velvet cheek. "I used to be very fond of dolls, and a live one would be so nice. I almost wish it was mine."

"Don't forget that you would be only half owner if it was," said Edward laughing. "But come now, my dear, it is time we were attending to dressing. The tea bell will ring directly."

"Well, I'll always want to share everything I have with you," she said. "Mamma," rising and putting her hand into her husband's, "we've had such a nice time! Ned has been so good and kind to me!"

"And she has been the best and dearest of little wives," he said, returning the look of fond affection she had bent upon him. "So we could not fail to enjoy ourselves hugely."

"I am rejoiced to hear it," Elsie said, looking after them with glad tears in her eyes as they left the room together.

The children were enjoying themselves greatly at the Oaks. Horace Dinsmore, Jr., and his young wife made a very pleasant host and hostess. Horace's reminiscences of his own childhood and his sister Elsie's girlhood in this, her old home, were very interesting—not to Rosie and Walter only, but to the others as well.

They were shown her suite of rooms, the exact spot in the drawing room where she stood during the ceremony that united her to Mr. Travilla, and the arbor—where he offered himself to her and was accepted.

They had an equally pleasant visit at the Laurels, whither they went directly from the Oaks. Gracie wondered why she was not permitted to go to see her mamma first for a while and grieved over it for a time.

They were not told what had taken place in their absence until the day of their return to Ion.

Mrs. Dinsmore had driven over for them and after an hour's chat with her daughter, Mrs. Lacey, sent for the children who were amusing themselves on the grounds.

"Oh, grandma, good morning! Did you come to take us home?" cried Rosie as she came running in, putting her arms about Mrs. Dinsmore's neck and holding her face up for a kiss.

"Yes, dear child, and to bring you some news. Good morning, Max, Lulu, Gracie, Walter—all of you—there's a little stranger at Ion."

"A little stranger!" was the great, simultaneous exclamation from all five. Max added, "What sort?" and Rosie, "Where from?"

"A very sweet, pretty little creature, I think. She's a little girl from 'No Man's Land,'" was the smiling reply. "A new little sister for you—Max, Lulu, and Gracie, a niece for Rosie and Walter."

Max looked pleased, though slightly puzzled, too. Gracie's eyes shone, and the pink flush deepened on her cheeks as she asked delightedly, "Is it a baby? Mamma's baby?" But Lulu only stood silently and frowned.

"Yes, children, it is your mamma's baby," replied Grandma Rose. "Would you like to go home and meet her?"

All answered in the affirmative except Lulu, who said nothing, as they all hurried from the room to make ready.

"Oh, Lu, aren't you glad?" exclaimed Gracie, as they put on their hats.

"No!" snapped Lulu. "What is there to be glad about? She'll steal all papa's love away from us. Mamma Vi's, too, of course, if she ever had any."

Gracie was shocked. "Lulu!" she said, just ready to cry. "How can you say such things? I just know nothing will ever make papa quit loving us. Can't he love us and the new baby, too? And can't Mamma Vi, too?"

"Well, you'll see!" returned Lulu wisely.

There was no time for any further exchange. The goodbyes were said, they were helped into the Ion carriage waiting at the door, and were driven rapidly homeward.

During the drive Grandma Rose noticed that while the other children were merry and talkative, Lulu was silent and sullen and Gracie apparently ready to burst into tears.

She more than half suspected what the trouble was, but deemed it best to seem not to see that anything was amiss.

Mr. Dinsmore and his daughter were on the veranda waiting to welcome the little party upon their arrival, and Rosie and Walter were well content to stay with their mother for a little while. The other three children immediately passed on up to Violet's rooms.

They found her in her boudoir, seated in an easy chair beside a window overlooking the avenue with her baby on her lap.

She was looking very young, very sweet and beautiful, very happy, too—though a shade of anxiety crossed her features as the children came in.

"How are you, dears? I am very glad to see you again," she said, smiling sweetly and holding out her pretty, white hand.

Gracie sprang forward with a little joyful cry. "Oh, mamma, my dear, sweet, pretty mamma! I am so glad to get back to you!" and threw her arms about Violet's neck.

Violet's arm was instantly around the child's waist. She kissed her tenderly two or three times, then said, looking down at the sleeping babe, "This is your little sister, Gracie."

"Oh, the darling, wee, pretty dear!" exclaimed Gracie, bending over it. "Mamma, I'm so glad, if—if—" She stopped in confusion, while Lulu, standing back a little, threw an angry glance at her.

"If what, dear?" asked Violet.

"If you and papa will love me and all of us just as well," stammered the little girl. She grew very red, and her eyes filled with tears.

"Dear child," Violet said, drawing her to her side with another tender caress, "you need not doubt it for a moment."

"Why, Gracie, what could have put such a notion in your head?" asked Max. With an affectionate glance at her, then a gaze of smiling curiosity at the babe, he queried, "Mamma Vi, may I kiss you and the baby, too?"

"Indeed, you may, Max," Violet answered, offering her lips.

"I'm glad she's come, and I expect to love her dearly," he remarked. When he had touched his lips softly to the babe's cheek, he said, "Though I'd rather she'd have been a boy, as I have two sisters already and no brother at all."

"Haven't you a kiss for me, Lulu, dear?" Violet asked entreatingly, "and a welcome for your new, little sister?"

Lulu silently and reluctantly kissed both, then turned and walked out of the room.

Violet looked after her with a slight sigh. But at that moment her own little brother and sister created a diversion by running in with a glad greeting for her and the new baby.

Their delight was rather noisily expressed, and no one of the little group either heard or saw a carriage drive up the avenue to the main entrance.

But Mr. Dinsmore and Elsie had been on the watch for it. They had been exchanging meaning, happy glances all morning and were ready with the warmest of greetings for the tall, handsome, noble-looking gentleman who hastily alighted from it and ran up the veranda steps.

"Dear mother!" he said, grasping Mrs. Travilla's hand, as he gave her a filial kiss.

"We are glad to see you, captain," she said. "Your telegram this morning was a delightful surprise."

"Yes, it was, indeed, to all of us who knew of its arrival," replied Mr. Dinsmore, shaking hands in his turn.

"My wife! How is she? And the children? Are they all well?" asked the gentleman breathlessly.

"All well," was the answer. "We told Violet you had reported yourself in Washington, and she will not be overcome at the sight of you. You will find her in her own rooms."

He hurried thither, met Gracie at the head of the stairs, and caught her in his arms with an exclamation of astonishment and delight.

"Can this be my own baby girl? This plump, rosy little darling?"

"Papa!" she cried, throwing her arms about his neck and hugging him tightly, while he kissed her again and again with ardent affection. "Oh, have you come? No, I'm your own little Gracie, but not the baby girl now, for there's a little one on mamma's lap. Come, and I'll show you."

"Ah!" he exclaimed, letting her lead him on. "I had not heard, as I have not had a letter for three or four weeks."

They were at the door. Gracie threw it open. Rose was holding the babe. Violet looked up, started to her feet with a cry of joy, and in an instant was in her husband's arms, weeping for very gladness.

For several moments they were conscious of nothing but the joy of the reunion. Then, with a sudden recollection she withdrew herself from his arms, took her babe, and laid her in them.

"Another darling," he said, gazing tenderly upon it. "Another dear, little daughter! My love, how rich we are!"

He kissed the babe, gave her to the waiting nurse, and turned to his wife again.

"Let me help you to the sofa, love," he said.

"Lie down for a little. I fear this excitement will exhaust and injure you."

She let him have his way. He sat down by her side, held her hand, and bent over her in sweet, loving anxiety.

"Are you quite well?" he asked.

"Very well indeed," she said, looking up fondly into his face. "And, oh, so happy now that you are here, my dear husband!"

Gracie crept to his side and leaned lovingly against him.

"My little darling," he said putting his arm round her and turning to give her a kiss. "But where are Max and Lulu?"

"Up in the boys' workroom, papa," she replied. "They don't know you've come."

"Then I must enlighten their ignorance," he said gaily. "Excuse me a moment, my love. Take care of mamma for me while I'm gone, Gracie," and rising hastily he left the room.

Max and Lulu were busily engaged looking over designs and materials for their work and discussing their comparative merits. So deeply interested were they that they took no note of approaching footsteps till they halted in the doorway. They turned their heads and saw their father standing there, regarding them with a proud, fond, fatherly smile.

"Papa! Oh, papa!" they both cried out joyfully and ran into his outstretched arms.

"My dear, dear children!" he said, holding them close and caressing first one, then the other.

He sat down with one on each knee, an arm around each, and for some minutes there was a delightful exchange of demonstrations of affection.

"Now you see, Lu, that papa does love us as well as ever," Max said, in a tone of triumph and satisfaction.

"Did she doubt it?" asked the captain in surprise, as he gazed searchingly into her face.

She blushed and hung her head.

"She thought the new baby would steal all your love," said Max.

"Silly child!" said her father, drawing her closer and giving her another kiss. "Do you think my heart is so small that it can hold love enough for a limited number? Did I love Max less when you came? Or you less when our heavenly Father gave Gracie to us? No, daughter, I can love the new-comer without any abatement of my affection for you."

"Papa, I'm sorry I said it. I won't talk so any more. And I mean to love the baby very much," she murmured with her arm about his neck, her cheek laid to his.

"I hope so," he said. "It would give me a very sad heart to know that you did not love your little sister, Lulu."

"Well, Max, my son, what is it?"

The boy was hanging his head and his face had suddenly grown scarlet. "Papa, I—I—did you get my letter and diary I sent you last month?"

"Yes, and Lulu's also," the captain said with a sigh and a glance from one to the other, his face growing very grave. "I think my children would often be deterred from wrong doing by the thought of the pain it would cause their father, if they could at all realize how sore it is. It almost broke my heart, Max, to learn that you had again been guilty of the dreadful sin of profanity and had learned to gamble, also. Yet, I was greatly comforted by the assurance that you were truly penitent, and hoped you had given your heart to God.

"My boy and my little girl, there is nothing else I so earnestly desire for you as that you may be His true and faithful servants all your days, His in time and eternity."

A solemn silence fell on the little group and for several minutes no one spoke.

Lulu was crying softly, and there were tears in Max's eyes, while the father held both in a close embrace.

At length Lulu murmured, "I am sorry for all my naughtiness, papa, and do mean to try very hard to be good."

"I, too," said Max, struggling with his emotion, "and if you think I deserve—oh, I know I do—and, papa, if you think you ought to—"

"You have had your punishment, my son," the captain said in a moved tone. "I consider it all sufficient. And now, we will go down to Mamma Vi and Gracie. I want you all together, that I may enjoy you all at once and as much as possible for the short time that I can be with you.

"But before I go, I have a word more to say. There is one thing about you both that greatly comforts me, my darlings. That is your truthfulness, your perfect openness with me, and your willingness to acknowledge your faults."

Those concluding words brought a flush of joy and love to each young face as they were lifted to his. He gave a hearty kiss to Lulu, then to Max, and led them from the room—a very happy pair.

Chapter Twenty-Fifth

One sacred oath has tied
Our loves; one destiny our life shall guide,
Nor wild, nor deep, our common way divide.

—Prior

Edward sat at the open window of his wife's boudoir enjoying the beauties of the landscape—the verdant lawn, the smiling field and wooded hills beyond, the sweet morning breeze and the songs of the birds—while Zoe in the adjacent room put the finishing touches on dressing.

She came to him presently, very simply dressed in white—looking sweet and fresh as a rose just washed with dew, and seated herself upon his knee.

"Darling!" he said, low and tenderly, putting his arm about her slender waist and imprinting a kiss upon the rosy cheek.

"My dear, dear husband! What would I ever do without you? How desolate I should be this day, if I hadn't you to love and care for me!" she said with a sob, stealing an arm round his neck and laying her cheek to his. "You know—I know you cannot have forgotten—that it is just one year today since dear papa died."

"Think what a blessed year and a happy meeting it has been to him, love, in that blessed land you may look forward to. There, death-divided friends will meet never to part again, free from sin and sorrow, pain and care, to be 'forever with the Lord.'"

"No, I have not forgotten what this day one year ago took from you, or what it gave to me—my heart's best treasure."

He drew her closer and touched his lips to hers.

"Oh, I'm very happy!" she said. "It has been a happy year in spite of my grief for my dear father, except—oh, Ned, we'll never be cross again, will we?"

"I trust not, my darling," he said. "It is too sharp a pain to be at variance with one's other half," he added, with playful tenderness. "Is it not, love?"

"Indeed, indeed it is!" she cried.

"See! This is to prove to you that I have not forgotten what a treasure I secured a year ago," he said, reaching for a jewel-case nearby.

"Pearls! Oh, how lovely! The most magnificent set I ever saw. Many, many thanks, dear Ned!" she exclaimed in delight. "I shall wear them this evening in honor of the day."

"But what shall I give you? I'm afraid I have nothing but—what I gave you a year ago—myself."

"The most priceless treasure earth can afford!" he responded, clasping her close to his heart.

"And your love," she said softly, her arm stealing round his neck again, as her shining eyes gazed fondly into his, "is more to me than all its gold and jewels."